saving the secret prince

a sweet romantic comedy

kristin canary

To my own Prince Charming
You may not have an actual title, but you have my heart.
Thank you for all of your love and support—and for putting
up with my musical tastes that veer so far from your own.

one

· · ·

THERE'S one thing you need to know about me—one very important detail that is much more important than who my mother is or what I do for a living or my last name.

Ready for it?

Here we go—

Oops. Got distracted there for a minute by the lyrics in my head. This happens more than you might think. Ahem.

Where was I? Right.

The thing you need to know about me is that I just might be the biggest lover of the '90s boy band 'N Sync who has ever existed.

That's right, I said it. Ever.

My eternal love of the Fab Five is how I find myself at the San Diego arena on a Friday night, cheeks wet and heart full. Despite being surrounded for the last three hours by thousands of screaming thirty-something women pretending like their hormones haven't yet regulated, I'm still sighing in sweet, sweet contentment. For one night and one night only, we have all been released from the bonds of the mid-life doldrums and allowed to act like total preteens drooling over the latest issue of *Teen Bop* magazine.

Because that's what happens when 'N Sync finally does the reunion concert you've been waiting for all your life.

After swiping away the tears of joy that rolled down my face during the closing number, I sling my arm around my housemate, Shelby Phillips. "That was the best thing ever. Forget marriage and babies—I think I can really and truly die happy now."

Her short blonde hair bobs as she shakes her head at me and smiles. "It was good, Lauren."

The noise level around us starts to die off as the audience continues its exit from the concert venue.

"Shelbs, that was not just good. That"—I gesture toward the now-deserted stage, where five of the best vocal talents in history just sang, danced, and made love to the crowd together—"was pure genius. Did you see when Justin flew in from above?

"You mean JT?"

"He will always and forever be only Justin to me." I place a hand over my heart dramatically. "They pretended like he couldn't make it and then BAM—there he was. It was magic."

Shelby grabs my hand and squeezes it. "It was fun seeing you so excited."

Once again, my twenty-five-year-old housemate has proven her sweet nature by letting me drag her to a concert she cares nothing about. Give her a good old-fashioned musical and she'd have the same giddy look I'm sure I'm wearing, but I guess pop music doesn't do it for her. "You're just too young to fully appreciate the glory that was Justin's bleached curly-sue locks or the thrill of learning the choreography to *Bye Bye Bye* behind the bleachers after school."

By this time, most of our row has cleared out. Next to me, the large dude with the surprisingly high-pitched falsetto who knew every single word of every single song (props to him, man) turns and shuffles out behind a green-haired female with a T-shirt featuring Joey Fatone's face. Her style hardly matches my own boring brown locks, skinny jeans, and green long-sleeved blouse, but that just proves how 'N Sync brings people together.

Le sigh. They really are the best.

We follow the lingering crowd off the main arena floor and into the hallway. "I need to stop at the restroom really quick if that's okay," Shelby says.

"Yeah, of course." The large windows of the arena show a gorgeous moon and twinkling stars outside. While Shelby slips into the restroom line, I pull my phone from my purse. Absently, I check my email. There's nothing much new, just a company-wide message from my boss, Jen, at New Heights Gym about holiday promotions we've got going on. Not surprising with Christmas only three weeks and one day away.

I get that familiar pinch in my chest, the one that

always comes when I think about the holidays and how far away my family is. About how that's my own choice, made out of necessity, survival.

In order to preserve who I am—who I want to be—I had to escape.

But that doesn't mean I don't think about my mom and sister, Samantha. That never stops. It's why I regularly stalk their social media pages.

Before I can stop myself, I navigate to the one social media site I'm a member of. The first thing I see is my own profile and a cascade of photos I've taken. Some women keep written diaries, but my journal is this digital photo album that no one else sees—because I don't allow any followers.

Flipping to Sam's page, I smile when I see a selfie of her cheek to cheek with her best friends at some sort of nightclub. She's cut her brown hair chin length and her eyes are done all smoky-like. In her mid-twenties, she's so beautiful, so full of life. Or that's how it appears in the photos, anyway.

I wish I knew for sure.

But after leaving the way I did, I don't have a right to ask for details about her life. We keep our relationship to occasional texting. That was my choice five years ago—and I don't know how to change it now. All I can do is pray that our mother hasn't dug her claws into Sam, that the independent streak I've always admired in my sister has held strong. That she hasn't let Mom's fame change her.

"Ready to go?"

I startle and nearly drop my phone at Shelby's

sudden appearance by my side. Clearing my throat, I shove my phone back into my purse. "Yep." Then I take off at a quick clip, as if I can escape the demons of my past.

"Whoa, you okay?" Shelby hurries to keep up as we dodge people—people everywhere.

"Of course." And why shouldn't I be? "We just experienced a once-in-a-lifetime event. I'm going to tell my kids about that concert." If I can ever meet a decent guy, that is. Not that I've really tried. Oh sure, I go on dates now and again, but nothing ever sticks.

After the fiasco with Danny, I'm not too eager to try again with someone new. Of course, next time I'll make sure I don't fall for some hotshot who's in the public eye.

We finally make our way past the long line of concertgoers waiting to buy merch and emerge into the crisp night air.

"Brr." Shelby tugs on her adorable pink trench coat and burrows down. "I know this is probably nothing compared with the East Coast, but this California girl is cold."

It used to be funny to me, how people here bust out the scarves and coats when it turns sixty-five out. Of course, San Diego is this strange SoCal pocket where things can get chillier than you might expect. But it's almost always *at least* fifty degrees around the holidays.

And while I do miss snow at Christmas, there's something about the sparkling sand of the beaches in winter that makes this feel more like home—more inviting—than New York ever did.

Now, the cold December air feels amazing on my skin after the proximity to so many bodies in the arena. Or maybe I'm still just heated from all my internal friction after seeing my sister's photo. Either way, I crave the open air and can't imagine climbing back into a vehicle right now. "How do you feel about a walk?"

Shelby's nose scrunches. "Like, right now?" She blows into her hands.

I link my arm with hers. "It's the weekend and the night is young. Come on. I'll keep you warm." Some might call me impulsive, but I like to think of it as seizing the day. "If I remember right, there's a cute coffee shop not that far from here. I'll buy you one of those fancy drinks you like." And get myself a hot chocolate.

"All right." The light from the many streetlamps illuminating the concrete and asphalt obscures the pretty sky. "But won't Josh and Kayla feel like you're cheating on Java Awakening?" she teases.

I laugh as we walk toward the sidewalk on the far end of the parking lot. "I think they'll understand. I've only been working there a week, after all."

"I don't know how you fit it all in. Gym instructor, teacher's aide, barista. You're like Superwoman."

Shrugging, I toss my hair over my shoulder. "The jobs pay the bills, and I like the variety."

Reaching the sidewalk, we turn north, away from the lengthy line of cars waiting to get on the main road that will take them to the freeway. Instead, we take the long way. It's not as populated with a bit less light, but we're together, so I'm not too worried about weirdos approaching us.

"So, how is it working with the newlyweds?" Shelby's teeth chatter slightly. "I am so happy for Kayla, but I wish we could have been at their wedding."

Kayla, one of our former housemates, showed up married last weekend after a Thanksgiving trip to visit her fiancé Josh's family in Oregon. Apparently they made a pit stop in Vegas after Josh's mom peppered her with questions about the wedding. That, plus the fact that a wedding is expensive—they just bought a house and Kayla is running a fledgling dating coach business—led to their decision to marry quickly.

I inhale, the scent of the ocean not far away. There are so many things I love about living here—the food, my friends, not to mention the freedom to be who I want to be without fear that it'll be documented and twisted—and the beach ranks high on the list. "I know, Shelbs. But Kayla and Josh are happy and that's all that matters, right?"

"Of course." A pause. "I hope someday to be as happy as them. And Evie and Connor, too."

Our other former housemate, Evie, is marrying her fiancé in two and a half weeks, just days before Christmas. We're all bridesmaids, and it's going to be beautiful. I can't wait to bust out my phone and take photos when no one is watching.

"You will. Keep the faith." Up ahead, I spot a lone man striding down the sidewalk toward us and talking on his phone—loudly—but he's too far away for me to hear what he's saying. A black hoodie is pulled over his head, obscuring his face in the dim light.

I return my attention to Shelby and try to effect a casual tone. "Who knows. Maybe we've already met the men we're going to marry and just don't know it yet."

All of us think Shelby and her best friend, Eric, would be perfect together. The only ones who don't seem to see it are Shelby and Eric themselves. But it always makes Shelby blush when we tease her about it, so I think there's more to the story.

"I—"

Shelby's comment is interrupted by the shouts of the man on the phone. Now he's stopped at a crosswalk and gesticulating wildly. A single car passes down the street, a reminder that this area is rather deserted. No one would hear us scream if the guy decided to turn and attack.

I halt, tugging on Shelby's arm. "Maybe we should go a different way."

"I'm sorry for leaving like that, all right?" The man— who is speaking in a delectable British-like accent—rubs his forehead and the hood of his sweatshirt falls away.

And darn it all if I don't lose feeling in my toes. Everything goes tingly and I feel like God must have spent a little more time on him, if you know what I'm saying. The harmony plays in my mind and I nearly break out into a song. Seriously.

Maybe it's the lamplight shining down on him, but he resembles some sort of sleek demigod—a savory Superman-slash-Thor sandwich.

I mean, sure, I can't see the exact details of his face,

except for a dark beard covering his square jaw and chiseled cheekbones, but there's something almost elegant about his posture. He commands attention and I wonder what other superpowers he might possess in addition to extreme hotness.

Thankfully, he doesn't notice my gawking. Doesn't notice Shelby or me at all, it seems.

Blowing out a breath, SuperThor rubs a hand along the back of his neck and stares at the street. "I just needed to get away for a bit."

Who is he talking to? A boss? A friend? Oh no. A girlfriend. Is it a girlfriend?

Of course it's a girlfriend. A man like THAT definitely has a girlfriend. Or wait, a wife. Is he wearing a ring? I look for a flash of gold or silver on his finger, but it's too dark.

Girl, you've officially lost it.

"Lauren," Shelby whispers. "Should we go?"

"Um—" Yes. Probably.

But before I can make a decision one way or another, it's made for me. SuperThor begins to cross the street.

Bye bye bye. I'll always remember you, SuperThor.

Shelby and I start walking again, but suddenly the road fills with headlights as a car careens around the corner.

And SuperThor just keeps chattering and yelling into his phone, apparently unaware that his life should be flashing before his probably-delicious eyes right about now.

I gasp, drop Shelby's arm, and sprint toward him like it's *my* life that depends on it. "Look out!"

At my shout, he turns to me. "What?" Then he sees the car and his eyes widen.

Just before the car connects with him—or me—I fling my body at him. We both fly toward the opposite sidewalk and land with an *oomph* as our heads knock together.

Tires squeal, and I should be concerned, but most of my attention is stuck on his eyes, the color of which I can't quite seem to grasp in the darkness. But they're piercing, I'll give him that.

"Are you all right, love?"

Love. He called me love. I laugh and inhale sharply. Wait, why am I giggling like a schoolgirl? But oh my gosh, he definitely came from heaven because the dude smells divine—like jasmine and cedar and bergamot and sandalwood, all wrapped up in one lovely package.

Merry Almost Christmas to me.

That's when I realize—why does my brain feel so stupidly slow?—that I'm lying on top of him on the asphalt.

"Sorry," I say, but I don't move. I'm not sure I can. My head is about to split into two.

"No worries." He shifts me gently so I'm level with him on the ground. One of his arms is still beneath my body and his eyes continue to study me. "Are you okay?"

Ambulance sirens whine in the background, getting louder and louder by the second. Why is there an ambulance? We're all fine here.

"Yep. Just fine. Fine, fine, fine." I lay my head down

against his Thor-like chest and snuggle into the crook of his arm. "I take back what I said. *Now* I can die happy."

I giggle again, but the laughter sends a sharp pain through my skull. "Ow." Then, I close my eyes.

The last thing I hear before everything goes black is the whisper of a promise—"No one's dying tonight, love."

two

· · ·

I OPEN my eyes to a flickering fluorescent light above me. My head hurts to look at it, so I squeeze my lids shut again.

"Lauren?" That would be Shelby.

I groan. "Is it about to rain or something?" Sometimes I get migraines in the few days before a storm, but this feels different, only localized to the forehead region.

"Hang on, let me get the doctor."

Doctor? My eyes fly open again and, after a few blinks, I take a good look around. I'm lying in a hospital bed surrounded by a wall on one side and a wraparound pink curtain on the other three. Shelby is just ducking out of sight before I can call to her again.

There's lots of beeping, but it's coming from some other corner of what I'm assuming is the hospital emergency room. Just beyond my curtained-off space, feet patter along the linoleum floor and people chatter in muted tones.

Sitting up, I wince a bit and run my hands along my arms, my torso, my legs. Nothing seems broken, thank goodness. So why am I here?

The car! The man! The ambulance ...

It all floods back.

Shelby returns with a handsome blond doctor in tow. "I was so worried about you." She gives me a quick hug.

"How long have I been here?"

"Not that long. Maybe thirty minutes? You woke up a few times in the ambulance."

"I did?" I definitely don't remember that.

"You most likely have a concussion," the doctor says. Shelby moves aside for him.

I squint at his name tag. "Dr. Ryan Rosche. You look familiar."

He takes one of those pen lights out of his pocket and smiles. "I believe I'm your neighbor."

Oh, that's right! We've all drooled over him when he jogs by our front window with his dog in the mornings. "Yes! I didn't recognize you with a shirt on." Yikes. Did I really just say that? I'm not the most filtered person in the world, but that sounded super flirtatious. And while he's good-looking, there just isn't the same spark I felt when I caught my first glimpse of SuperThor. This head trauma must be worse than a simple headache. What did he say? A concussion? "I mean ..."

Thankfully, he gives a deep chuckle. "Let's get you checked out, all right, Ms. Everly?"

"It's Lauren." Even though I go by Lauren Smith when I introduce myself, all of my official documentation still has my actual name. I looked into changing it when I moved here five years ago for anonymity's sake, but it didn't seem wise to spend the little money I had on something symbolic.

He takes a while to do a full workup, then says he wants to keep me in the ER for a bit to observe me. If all is well, he will send me home with instructions to take it easy for the next few days.

When he leaves, Shelby comes over and grabs my hand. "You're a hero, you know."

I am? Oh! "Is SuperThor all right?"

"SuperThor?" Shelby's lips twitch.

I gesture her comment away. "The one I pushed? Is he okay?"

"At the scene, he seemed fine other than some scrapes on his face."

Breathing out a sigh of relief, I slump back against the pillows. There's nothing more I want to do than allow myself to slip back into sleep. "That's good." Oh wait! I sit up again. "I need to call Jen and let her know I won't be in tomorrow."

"I already did that for you. I got her voicemail, though, so hopefully she'll get the message before your first cycling class tomorrow."

"You're the best."

She tilts her head. "Evie, Kayla, and Alexis are all in the waiting room and dying to see you. They'll only let one of us back at a time. Guess I should relinquish my turn." But despite her words, she keeps holding onto my hand.

"Thank you for being here." I pause, taking her in. Is

that a glisten in her eyes or is my injured head playing tricks on me? "You okay?"

"I just hate hospitals." She swallows. "Hate seeing people I love inside them."

Her mom was really sick when Shelby was young and died from a terrible genetic disease. Losing a parent is something we've bonded over, since I lost my dad to a construction worksite accident when I was just a toddler. Sadly I don't even remember him, but Shelby has years of memories with her mom—which honestly, probably makes it harder for her than me. Or maybe just hard in a different way.

I squeeze her hand. "You heard the doctor. I'm going to be completely fine."

Shelby nods as she white knuckles my fingers. "Right. Okay." Bending down, she kisses my cheek and leaves to fetch one of our other friends.

I settle back against the pillows when I hear a commotion nearby. The sound of a curtain being flung open—metal rings clattering against a rod—meets my ears. It's close, maybe in the bay next to mine.

Then, "You look awful."

The voice, it's deep and British-sounding. But I don't know it.

"Thanks a load. You look fairly terrible yourself."

But *that* voice—that one I recognize. At least, I think I do. Is that SuperThor?

"Whose fault is that? If I hadn't been trying to locate you when you ran off—"

"I told you. I just needed some air. Alone. Try to understand."

"And just what am I going to tell your parents?" Now the first voice is tinged with anger. Or is that worry? And why would he have to tell SuperThor's parents anything?

"Tell them nothing."

I lean sideways because it seems like the voices have gotten fainter, and I am suddenly very invested in the soap opera unfolding before me—er, beside me?

"They're going to know when they see the hospital bill arrive."

His parents pay his bills still? That's a bit disappointing. Maybe he still lives with them. That *should* greatly reduce his attractiveness—although, let's be honest. That just lowers him to a ten, because the dude was probably like a seventeen or eighteen already.

Fine. Twenty. He's freaking double the norm. Demigod, remember?

"My parents don't handle such paltry affairs."

"You're so stubborn. At least I could get you better accommodations than *this*." A pause. "Simply say the word and I'll tell the doctors—"

"That's not necessary. I'm fine here, and I'm sure I'll be leaving as soon as the paperwork's ready."

My phone buzzes on my bedside tray. I lunge to silence it so I can hear the rest of the men's conversation next door, but don't anticipate how my legs have gotten tangled in the sheets.

Annnnnd now I'm hanging half in the bed, half out of it. I'm an upside-down Jack in the box, and my head starts spinning.

Naturally, Kayla sweeps into my bay at that exact

moment. Rushing to me, she helps me sit up. "What is happening here, Lauren?"

My cheeks flush and I close my eyes to still the room now that I'm upright again. "I tried to get my phone because someone was calling me. And I … fell."

After a few seconds, Kayla speaks. "Looks like there's a voicemail from Jen Flanigan. That's your boss at the gym, right?"

"Yeah." I hold out my hand, but Kayla doesn't slip me the phone.

I peek at her and she's got the phone to her ear. "What are you doing?"

"Shh." She waves me off, then plugs one ear, clearly listening to the message. How does the woman even know my passcode? She used to be a lawyer, so I guess it makes sense she's so observant.

For the first time, I realize her highlighted brown hair is pulled back into a ponytail, unusual for someone who always wears it down and styled. She's also dressed in flannel pajama pants and a black T-shirt that says Best Wife in the Galaxy in the *Star Wars* font. That sets off my giggles again.

This woman—who has always been the chicest among us, with her tight dresses and Prada heels—has allowed her inner nerd out ever since Josh came into her life. I love how he's softened her rough edges, helped her be okay with expressing herself, helped her trust again.

Maybe someday I'll meet a man who can do that for me.

I don't even bother protesting that she's stolen *my* phone and is listening to *my* voicemail, because that's just Kayla for you. And she may have changed in some ways since Josh, but there's nothing and no one on the planet able to make her less bossy. She's just a take-charge kind of person, but she also loves and protects fiercely.

Her expression hardens as she listens. After what seems like ages, she lowers the phone.

"What did she say?" I bunch the hospital bed's top sheet in my fist.

Kayla begins pacing. She doesn't have much space in my little corner of the ER, so she's basically taking three steps then turning to take three more. It's honestly exhausting to watch. "Apparently last year a personal trainer got into an accident of some sort, was seen in the ER, and decided to come back to work despite medical advice. Then he was re-injured on the job and sued the company when they wouldn't pay workman's comp, since the initial injury didn't occur at work." She halts and lifts an eyebrow in my direction to make sure I'm following. "In the end, even though he probably wouldn't have won the lawsuit, the company settled with him."

I scrunch my nose. "What does that have to do with me?"

"I'm getting to that. Since that time, corporate's legal team has developed a new policy. Any unsalaried employees with non-desk jobs who have been seen in the ER, no matter how minor their injuries, must take two weeks of unpaid leave and must have a doctor's note at the end of those two weeks to show they can return to work."

"Wait. What?" Did I hear her right? Two weeks of unpaid leave? "But I need that job!"

"I know."

"I mean, I just got the job at the coffee shop because you and Evie moved out and Alexis is hesitant to take on new housemates, which means the rent is higher for each of us …" Despite being hourly, the gym is my best-paying job, and the place I work at twenty-five to thirty hours a week. The coffee shop is about ten hours, and I only work the teacher's aide job once a week for eight hours. I lick my lips as I calculate how much money I'll be out if I can't work for two weeks.

It's a lot.

And now, not only will I not have enough for food and rent, but these hospital bills won't be cheap considering I don't have health insurance.

"Do you think Josh would be able to give me more hours at the coffee shop?"

"I can ask, but he just hired on another new girl to help with the holiday rush." Kayla taps her chin. "What about your teacher's aide job? You're only there once a week. Can they give you more hours?"

"No, I asked before I sought out the barista position."

"Well, I'm sure Alexis can waive your rent for the month. Her job pays well enough. Or I can loan you some money. My business is booming as of late. Or hey! You can have my hours at Java for the next few weeks."

"No." I won't take advantage of people, especially

my friends. It's just not how I ever want to treat people. Not when I know what it feels like.

"Don't be stubborn, Lauren."

"I'm not being stubborn." I pause. "I'll just find another job to fill in the blanks."

"Most everyone has already hired their holiday help." Kayla crosses her arms over her chest. "If only that idiot you saved had had the good sense to watch where he was going, none of this would have happened."

At that moment, the curtain dividing our bay from the next one over slides open. My jaw drops to see SuperThor sitting on the edge of the bed, his legs so long they are set firmly on the ground. There are a few small bandages on his forehead and neck. He's discarded the black hoodie and now just wears a white fitted T-shirt that shows off his muscled arms and defined chest—the chest I now remember snuggling against like we'd been dating for weeks instead of, you know, just having met.

"Um." I raise my hospital bed to a sitting position. "Hi."

"Good evening." How does he make two such mundane words sound so darn sexy?

It's the accent. It has to be the accent.

Kayla stalks over and grabs the edge of the curtain. "Excuse me. This is a private conversation. Just who do you think you are?"

"I believe you might know me as the idiot who wasn't watching where he was going."

Though he says it in a very straightforward way—no

hint of teasing in his tone or expression—I snort at his self-deprecation. The look of disbelief on Kayla's face has me smiling so hard my face hurts.

Or maybe the ache in my forehead is merely gravitating downward.

"I see." Kayla releases the curtain and lets it fall to the ground again. She waits for a few beats before asking, "And do you have a name other than Idiot?"

The corded veins in his arm seem to pop. "My friends call me Topher. Topher James. And this"—he hooks a thumb backward toward a man who steps from the shadow like some sort of spy—"is my … friend. Frederick."

"Pleasure." Frederick, a rather buff dude with a high-and-tight who seems about the same age as Topher —mid-thirties, if I had to guess—was definitely the first voice I heard before Kayla came in.

"I'm Lauren and this is Kayla," I manage. My throat is suddenly super dry.

Kayla shoves a clear cup into my hand and I drink, the cold water like a river flowing in the desert.

"We owe you a debt of gratitude," Frederick continues. "Thank you for saving His Ro—"

"Me. For saving me." Topher shoots his friend a look that I wouldn't want to be on the receiving end of. What had the guy been about to say that would warrant that kind of censure?

He looks at Kayla. "And you're right. I should have been paying more attention."

His focus snags on me and I chug more water because, DANG, does his gaze sear me like a finely grilled steak. "I deeply apologize for putting you in harm's way."

I hand the empty cup back to Kayla. "I kind of did that to myself."

"Still, if I hadn't been … well, never mind all that." He furrows his brow and studies me for several long moments, and I can't help but get a good look at the utter symmetry of his face. There's also the strong curve of his nose to consider, the green of his eyes that are just one or two shades darker than my favorite flavor of ice cream—mint chocolate chip. His beard isn't as thick as it looked in the dim light. It's more like manscaped scruff.

Everything about this man is well managed. He seriously is like some sort of chiseled masterpiece—one I wouldn't mind looking at on the regular.

Stop staring like a creeper, Lauren.

Oh, yeah. Hopefully he attributes any of my weird or awkward behavior to the head injury. I glance away and find Kayla looking at me. She lifts an eyebrow like she knows exactly what I'm thinking.

She probably does—the blasted mind reader.

Then she turns back to Topher. "So what are you going to do to make this right?"

"I was just about to get to that." A pause. "Of course, I will be paying for all of your hospital bills and any resulting medical bills you may incur."

Incur? Who talks like that? "That's really not necessary."

"Actually, it is." Kayla whips her phone out of who knows where—her bra?—and starts typing something into it. "And what about the loss of income she's about to endure? The pain and the suffering? I'm her lawyer, by the way."

I roll my eyes at my friend. "He doesn't need to do anything about all of that. I'm fine." I look over at Topher again. "Really."

He nods thoughtfully. "No, your lawyer is correct. I am happy to also pay any loss of income."

"I'm drawing up a contract right now," Kayla says.

But this is all going too fast, too far. I grip my head and shake it. "No, no, no. You can pay for the hospital bills. That will be fine. I'll find another way to make up the income."

"I really don't mind. The money isn't a problem."

Must be nice. But no, I've had money—I've seen what it plus fame can do to people. I'm happy living my quiet life paycheck to paycheck if it means I get to be me. "Seriously. It's okay."

"Why don't *you* hire her if you've got so much money lying around?" Kayla interjects, pointing at Topher. "She normally teaches cycling and a few other classes, but she's also a great personal trainer."

Yikes, no. Even though I'm technically still certified, I've never really been a personal trainer for any length of time. Sure, I teach strength training classes, but it's a bunch of little old ladies who attend, not big muscly men who would require—and want—a very different sort of instruction.

I open my mouth to say as much when Topher looks back at Frederick and then at me again. "All right. If that's what it will take to make this right. I'll hire you. Would two hundred an hour be sufficient?"

My jaw drops because, um, hello, that's way too much money. "Actually—"

Kayla thrusts her hand on her hip. "Make it two-fifty and *maybe* we won't sue you."

Topher sputters. "I don't—"

I shoot Kayla a glare. "No one is suing anyone."

Topher's shoulders immediately relax. For someone as well off as he seems to be, he sure was nervous about being sued. But no one likes to have their name dragged through the mud.

And I certainly have no desire to put myself back in the public eye. Never again, thank you very much.

I continue. "It was my decision to jump in front of that car, not his."

"As your lawyer, I advise you not to say another word." Kayla lifts her eyebrow, and gives me her scariest power look. But with the outfit she's wearing, it loses a bit of its effect.

"Good thing you're here as my friend and not my lawyer."

She mutters something under her breath as she plops onto the bed at my feet.

I turn to Topher and Frederick, who are eyeing me warily. "If you pay my hospital bills, I call that more than even. In fact, it's very generous of you." He may be a stranger to me, but I still won't take advantage of his kindness.

Finally, he speaks, his voice warmer somehow. A bit gentler. "I really do insist. You must allow me to help you in any way I can."

And whew, if that sexy accent doesn't have me practically drooling …

It's not just the accent, though, because Frederick's doesn't give me the same butterfly effect. It's the way Topher is talking to me like he actually cares—not just because he's taking responsibility for my injuries.

"I have to warn you. I haven't actually had much experience training others one on one." Try none. I took the PT course and exam only to satisfy a requirement at the gym, but never actually put it into practice afterward.

"That's all right."

Why is he so eager to help me? He must want to assuage his conscience, and since I can't seem to convince him that he doesn't need to, maybe we can help each other out.

And, I mean, I wouldn't exactly object to being in his majestic presence again—even if it's in a professional capacity.

Chewing my lip, I nod. "Okay, I guess I'll be your personal trainer." Not that the man needs it in any way. Heck, he could probably personally train me.

Now there's an idea …

Focus, Lauren. Atta girl.

He looks at Frederick with his eyebrows lifted.

Frederick reaches into his pocket and pulls out a card with a phone number—just a phone number—printed on it. Maybe he really is a spy. Either that or he's the most prepared friend in the world. Or could be they work together, because that definitely seemed like a boss-slash-employee move. But Topher called them friends, so I'm probably just imagining it.

Topher grabs the card from Frederick, then steps off the bed and into my bay to place the card in my hand. Our fingers brush, and it's like the lights above us are dancing a jig to the Hallelujah Chorus.

Or it's entirely possible that I'm seeing spots and my concussion is growing worse.

Or maybe there's just something about Topher ... something different. Something I can't put my finger on. He carries himself differently than other guys I've met—and working at a gym, I meet a lot of guys. They swagger and joke and flirt, and he's not doing any of those things.

But there *is* a certain confidence to him, a charisma that's magnetic.

"Call me in a week when you're feeling better and we'll set something up. That is, if you don't mind coming to me?"

Kayla starts to protest, but I hold up a hand to stop her. "Kay."

Rolling her eyes, she stands. "Do what you want. I'm going to go get Alexis. She called dibs on seeing you next."

Then, after doing the sign for "I'm watching you"—pointing her index and middle fingers first at her eyes and then at Topher's, a severe frown on her lips—she flounces out, leaving my curtain flapping in the breeze of her exit.

I can't help but chuckle at my overprotective friend.

She may be married and living somewhere else these days, but I know she will always have my back.

Topher clears his throat and I startle. Right. I haven't answered him. "I don't mind coming to you. And I'll probably be fine in a few days."

His terse nod reminds me of an army general. "I'm sure your doctor told you this, but do be sure to rest a lot. No alcohol or caffeine, screen time, that kind of thing. Oh, and you most definitely should avoid bright lights and loud noises."

I smile at his serious expression. "Are you a doctor or something?" Or maybe he's had a lot of concussions in his lifetime. He's certainly built like an athlete.

He shrugs. "I just read quite often."

For some reason, that makes me laugh—which in turn, makes Topher stiffen. Maybe he thinks I'm making fun of him. I hope not. Although it is kind of funny, because who reads doctor-y textbooks if they're not a medical professional?

"Okay, I'll text you in a few days."

Before I can say more, Alexis rushes in, her pink hair pulled into a braid. It's so bright, it hurts my eyes to look at it.

Hands on her hips, my landlord—and friend—pushes her lips to the side and scowls. "Lauren."

"Lexi Lou."

She growls at my nickname for her. "What were you thinking, jumping in front of a car like that? That was so dumb!"

I know it's love that's really speaking here. She just doesn't know how to show it like a normal human being. (The guy who cracks that nut is going to be a lucky man—because deep down, Alexis is really a puddle of goo.)

I turn to introduce Topher to Alexis, but the curtain has been released back into place. So I hold out my arms toward my friend. "Aw, I love you too."

Huffing, she bends over and wraps me in a hug. Just like the rest of my friends, she is a sister of my heart—part of the family I've chosen.

And I will never do anything to jeopardize that.

That's why I refuse to slouch in paying my rent. And it's also why, as soon as I am able, I will make my way to Topher's house and pretend like I know a little something about personal training.

three

. . .

WHEN TOPHER SAID money wasn't an issue, the dude meant it.

Four days after the accident, my jaw drops as my car rounds its final bend. Outside my window is the most gorgeous beachside neighborhood I've ever seen. I've been driving along the highway for a while now toward Del Mar, one of the ritzier parts of the larger San Diego area, and now that I've arrived at the destination Topher texted me yesterday, I wonder if my head is fully recovered or if this is really where he lives.

But as I pull up to a private gate with a security guard station, I double-check the address against the text.

Sure enough, this is the right place. A sign informs me that I've reached the Grand Cove Estates, and just beyond the guard station, I can see that there truly are grand homes here. Some are large, some are small, but each one just screams wealth, as do the Bentleys,

Porsches, and Mercedes parked in front of them. Every lawn is manicured to perfection, and many of them back the beach, which apparently is private. Yep, you heard that right—a private beach. In California. Do you know how much money that must cost?

Even though my mom is well off now, it wasn't always like that. We had a fairly normal childhood in Texas, of all places, but moved to New York so Mom could pursue her dreams when I was in middle school. That's when everything changed, although Mom didn't get her own television show until after my "accident."

Not the accident that just happened with Topher.

The other one.

I lower my window and wave to the security guard, a rather plump woman with fire-red hair growing in a frizzy ball around her head. She's got a baton and taser clipped to her belt. Overkill, much? Clearing my throat, I offer a smile. "Hi there. I'm a guest of Topher James's." I rattle off the address.

Red obviously takes her job very seriously, because she doesn't even return my smile—just grunts and turns back to her computer where she clicks around for a full thirty seconds. Finally, she raises the gate, walks back out to me, and points up a short hill. "Go one street that way and it's on the left."

Placing her hands on her belt, she huffs up her large chest and tilts her head at me. One curl of her Ronald McDonald hair that's longer than the rest bobs in the wind. "And ma'am, make sure you follow every law— or the law will follow you."

I don't know whether to gulp or laugh, so I eke out

some combined response and press the gas much harder than I mean to. The engine revs and Red shouts something at me as I drive away, praying she doesn't chase me down and tase me before I get to see the deliciousness that is Topher James again.

Because yeah, I may have spent one too many minutes dreaming of being in his arms once more (preferably this time because he chose it—ha!). Not that I expect that to happen. I'm just a regular girl working as his personal trainer. And even though I don't have terrible self-confidence issues, I'm not suave or sophisticated. I'm just fun, impulsive Lauren, and I'm guessing a man as stoic and upright as Topher James would prefer someone much more poised than I ever will be.

But that didn't stop me from blasting 'N Sync love ballads all the way here.

After following the guard's instructions, I'm in front of one of the smaller homes in the community. I climb from my rusty little Ford, breathing in the briny scent and relishing the ocean breeze on my cheeks that never gets old. The house is all square angles and glass, with windows that take up entire walls. I tuck my car keys into my purse and haul myself up the short walkway to the massive door.

Topher answers my knock almost immediately and once again I nearly swallow my tongue. Today he's in a purple workout tank that's doing wonders for his amazing arms and those dreamy eyes, as well as black athletic shorts that hit just above his tan, quite muscular knees. (And yes, knees can be muscular. You'll just have to trust me on this one.) The bandages from the hospital are gone, leaving a few scratches in their place. He's basically exactly as I remember him.

But the one thing that doesn't compute with my image of him? He's holding a massive book in his hand.

"Ms. Smith." He steps back from the doorway and gestures inside. "Come in."

"Hi. And um, it's Lauren."

"All right. Lauren."

It would be bad if I asked him to make a recording of my name so I could listen to it at night before I fall asleep each night, right?

Yes, Lauren, that would be next-level stalkerish.

Dang it. I hate it when my subconscious is right.

Once again, I'm met with his manly scent as I move past him into a posh living room with a modern vibe going on. The furniture is sleek and white, and everything else is accented black—from the tiled fireplace to the zebra-striped throw pillows. This isn't exactly the way I'd have expected him to decorate, but then again, what do I really know about him except that his picture belongs on the cover of *World's Most Gorgeous Men* magazine? (Is that a real thing? Because I'm totally subscribing if so!)

Well, I do know one other thing. He's kind. After all, he didn't have to agree to this arrangement, but he wanted to be sure I had the money I needed for rent.

Or maybe he's just super responsible or hates being in others' debt.

He places his tome on the glass coffee table, and I barely make out the title. *The History of Parasailing.* What a strange book to be reading. Besides, is there really *that much* to say about parasailing?

He catches me staring at the book. "The home gym is this way." Topher heads down the hallway and I scurry to follow, my purse banging against my side.

Before I make it to the room at the far end of the hall, though, I catch sight of the view from the kitchen. Gasping, I veer closer. Like others, this wall is entirely made of glass, letting in an abundance of light and showcasing the white sand below. There's no one out there—a rare thing for any beach in this town—and I immediately crave the feeling of sand between my toes and the sun on my face.

"Are you coming?"

I jump at Topher's voice, but grow still the moment he is standing beside me. Glancing up at him, I nod. "Just had to make a detour." I pause and sigh. "If I lived here, I'd be out there every day. Every moment."

"I normally don't have time for that kind of idleness, though it's been forced on me as of late."

Hey, now. "It's not idleness to enjoy nature and all its glory." And what does he mean, forced upon him? Not by me, I hope?

"But it's not productive either."

"Life is about more than productivity." I shake my head at him. "It's not healthy to live and breathe work alone." My mother is proof of that.

"That's not really a choice for me." His voice sounds far off, almost wistful, as he places his fingers against the glass and stares out at the frolicking waves.

"Everyone has a choice," I say quietly. "That's the only reason I'm standing with you right now. A choice."

Silence bends and wraps us up in the moment for one, two, three. Then he blinks. His hand drops as he steps back. "Well, shall we get to our training session so you can be on your way?"

He's trying to get rid of me already? Maybe he thinks I'm annoying. Or maybe he really is just a busy guy whose life I completely interrupted by agreeing to this deal.

"This way." He turns and marches down the corridor again, as if he just expects me to obey like a puppy. But perhaps he doesn't realize how … commanding he sounds.

As I follow, I pass Frederick, who is exiting one of the bedrooms. Maybe they're roommates? "Good morning, Ms. Smith."

What is with all the decorum around here? We're, like, the same age. Maybe in Britain or wherever they're from, it's a sign of respect, but it's just not me. I'm the very opposite of formal. "How's it going, Freddy?"

"Freddy, eh?" He grins at me, and today there's a bit more of a boyish air to him. Likely he was just worried for his friend the last time we met. He leans over like he's about to impart some secret. "You may wish to know that your trousers appear to be … reversed."

My eyes widen as I glance down at my yoga pants. Eek, he's right. The seams are on the outside, which means the tagless label in the back is probably showing too since my workout tank just barely meets the waistband. I groan. So much for making a good impression on Topher.

Oy vey. My subconscious is most definitely plotting against me—that or the fact that I got dressed way too quickly after sleeping in this morning. "Is there somewhere I can change?"

But at that moment, Topher's head pops out of a room. "Everything's all ready in here. Oh, hello, Frederick."

"Topher." Frederick's eyes sparkle as he winks at me and gestures me onward.

Guess Topher gets to see me in all my hot mess glory. Squaring my shoulders, I enter the room at the end of the hall, where he's standing on a blue mat. The outside window once again gives a lovely view of the coast. Along another regular white wall, there's a rack of free weights, as well as jump ropes, resistance bands, and a range of balance balls in various sizes. On another are a stationary bike, a treadmill, and a bench press.

I whistle. "This is like a gym rat's personal brand of heaven."

"Yes, it's quite extensive."

Lifting my eyebrows, I laugh.

He narrows his gaze at me. "What?"

"Sorry, I just keep forgetting that you're not from around here originally." I walk toward the free weights and run my finger along the sleek curves. "How long have you lived in San Diego?"

"I don't. Just here on holiday." His voice is tense, tight.

He doesn't live here? Boo.

I clear my throat. "You don't sound that happy about it."

"Like I said. It was forced on me."

"A vacation was forced on you? You really *must* be a workaholic." I flash him an impish grin. "So where do you live? England?"

He rubs the back of his neck. "A small island near there."

"What's it called?"

"I'm only here another few weeks." Now he just sounds exasperated—and he's very obviously ignoring my question. But why? "Can we begin now, please?"

"Of course." Sheesh, the man needs to lighten up. My friends always tease me about being a ball of positivity and energy, so maybe I can help him have a little fun.

I peruse the assortment of equipment and consider my options. "Hmm, where to start?"

Now, you'd think with three days lying around recovering from a head injury that really didn't end up being that major, I'd have taken the time to prepare for this moment. And truly, I meant to. I even had half a text message typed out to one of the personal trainers at my gym to ask for some tips.

But after I slept the day away on Saturday, my friends brought me various forms of entertainment. I said I'd just watch something on TV, but Kayla reminded me that I wasn't supposed to use screens. Together, she and Alexis hid the remote and my laptop from me like I was a toddler with no self-control.

I'm not saying it's an *untrue* assessment, but it still wounded my pride just a tad.

That left me with the stack of books Evie brought by—all advanced copies of historical romances that her publishing company is releasing in the next few months—or the audiobooks that Shelby recommended. Since it takes me forever to read a book the usual way, *The Lunar Chronicles* audiobooks won out. And that's how I spent the last forty-eight hours—not coming up with a plan for training Topher, but listening to four gripping stories while eating my weight in chocolate ice cream and Cheetos. (Don't judge me—I was injured!)

Which all means that right now, the quizzical look Topher gives me is completely justified. "Didn't you create a list of exercises or something along those lines?"

"I'm more of a decide-as-you-go kind of person. I don't like to be limited by lists."

He coughs. "Lists don't have to be restraining. They help you formulate a plan."

"The keys to success are planning, forethought, and worry. A well-placed worry makes all the difference." My mother's voice invades the moment.

Just as I always do, I push her advice aside—not because I don't love her, but because I don't want to become her.

"That's not really my style." I select some fifty-pound dumbbells and walk them to Topher. "Let's start with some basic bicep curls."

He eyes the weights. "Don't you want me to warm up on the treadmill first?"

"Oh, right." I throw some finger guns at him and

make two annoying clicking sounds like it's amateur hour. What is happening to me? I am normally super chill, yo. "Of course I do. Ha ha, I was just testing you. To see how much you knew already." Charging toward the treadmill, I pat the arm. "Hop on up here, Tiger."

Someone just shoot me now. I cannot fathom why these things are coming out of my mouth except that it's possible my brain short-circuited during the accident and hasn't fully recovered.

Topher just gives me a strange look and obeys. "How long should I go for?"

"Um, let's say ten minutes."

He starts the treadmill and soon is jogging. And whew buddy, there's just something about watching him move that's making *me* sweat. He's not even going that fast, but his whole body is like a powerhouse, a machine that's beautiful and bold all at once.

Gah. Needing a distraction, I hop up on the bike and do my own thing for the remainder of the time. Here is where I feel at home and comfortable. It's not like being a fitness instructor has always been my dream, but it's something I'm good at and enjoy.

Soon the time is up. My endorphins are flowing and I've got a renewed pep in my step. Who cares that I've been falling all over myself like a crazy woman or that my pants are inside out or that I have no clue what I'm doing?

I've got this.

Topher hops off and swipes at a thin layer of sweat beading on his forehead. "Now the bicep curls?"

Does the man ever stop? He really is a machine. In

some ways, he reminds me of Alexis, who keeps her emotions close to the vest and likes things to be a particular way. But Alexis loves me and I'm determined that Topher will too. (Well, not *love me* love me. You know what I mean.)

"Yep, let's do that," I say.

We both make our way to the weights I left on the ground. Oh right. I need to demonstrate—even though given his impressive physique, I'm fairly certain he knows how to use dumbbells.

Heading back to the free weights, I select some thirty pounders and then demonstrate the desired move. "See, nice and simple. Fluid. Lift the chest and head, and keep your back straight." I place the dumbbells back on the ground. "You want to make sure you're keeping your elbows tight to your sides, which will help ensure you're just using your biceps."

Before I can think about what I'm doing, I place a hand on his left bicep—as if he doesn't know what a bicep is. And man, oh man, the feel of his rock-hard muscle beneath my fingers is tearin' up my heart in all the best ways. "Wow."

No, you did NOT just say that out loud, girlfriend.

Oh, but I did. I really did.

He clears his throat and maintains his stiff posture.

Oh-kay, clearly he is seeing what a bad idea this whole personal training thing was, right? He's going to fire me if I don't get. it. together. I step away and gesture toward his fifty-pound weights. "Sorry, um, all right. Your turn."

And there, quick, one corner of his mouth turns

upward. And ladies and gentlemen, let me present Exhibit A (or B or C or … you get the picture) on why he's the most attractive man on the planet—because Topher James has a dimple on his right cheek.

And I don't even care that it makes him less than symmetrical, because it's pure perfection.

"I know you said you didn't have much experience, but just how many clients *have* you trained?" he asks.

I cough and wave my hand. "Hundreds. Thousands." Shoot, I'm caught if the widening of his smile is any indication. At least he doesn't seem mad. "Why do you ask?"

"No reason." He shakes his head, the ghost of a smile still there as he lifts the weights I've given him and does a set of fifteen reps without breaking a sweat.

Oh. That's why he asked. "You need a higher weight, don't you?"

Topher walks the weights back to the rack, then turns and taps the side of his nose. "By George, I think she's got it."

"Wait." I follow him, a silly grin suddenly plastered on my face. "Did you just crack a joke, SuperThor?"

"I'm sorry, SuperThor?"

Whoops. "Inside joke. You had to be there." Except he *was* there. (Ya'll, my brain is a scary place.)

"Uh-huh." Then he rubs his hands together, his eyes twinkling just slightly. "All right, what else do you have for me? I could lift weights like this all day."

Is he … teasing me? Because if so, I'm here for it.

"Laugh it up, buddy." My eye catches on the resistance bands, which I use all the time for my strength training classes. I snag a few and toss one his way. "I may not be up on all the latest weightlifting techniques for men, but I'm going to have you crying like a little baby when I'm done with you."

Okay, maybe not, but it's way too fun to tease him back. And, believe it or not, resistance bands can be trickier than they look, though I'll be kind and start him off with a rather simple move.

"Bring it on, Tiger."

I grin at his use of my earlier, ridiculous nickname for him. "Oh, I will." I loop the resistance band under my foot, keeping my eyes on Topher the whole time. He copies me. "We're going to start with a single-arm tricep move. Very simple. See if you can keep up."

I tug upward on the band like I've done a thousand times before—and the game is over because it slips out from under my foot. The end launches up and smacks me in the face. Crying out, I keel over and clutch my nose, which as it turns out, is gushing blood. "Ow, ow, ow."

"Whoa, love. Steady." Topher's hands are on my upper arms and his voice is gentle. How is he this calm? A complete mess of a woman is sitting before him bleeding all over his floor. "Pinch your nose and look up just a bit, but not too much or the blood will go down your throat."

Gross. I do what he says. "Did you read this in a book too?" My words are nasally and muffled. *Sexy.* Despite my attempt at humor, I actually kind of want to cry right now.

Can someone die from mortification? Because if so, then it's gonna be me.

"I had a lot of nosebleeds as a child." He gently angles my chin this way and that to inspect the damage. "Doesn't look like the band caught you anywhere but the nose. And I'm no expert, but it doesn't appear to be broken. There's some swelling though, so you might want to get it checked out by a doctor. You might have some bruising as well."

Wonderful. "Hopefully that's cleared up before the wedding."

"Wedding?" He tilts his head. "You're engaged?"

And I know it's not disappointment I hear in his voice—it can't be—but he does seem to back out of my air space just a tad.

"Oh no, not me. I'm a bridesmaid in my friend Evie's wedding in a few weeks."

And then, like the last few pieces of Skittles falling out of one of those turn-dial dispensers, more words spill from my mouth. "I'm free. Available. Not tied down." I wince. "I mean, I don't have a fiancé. Or a boyfriend for that matter."

Oh. My. Gosh. Stop talking, Lauren! Get off the Hot Mess Express right now!

"Noted." Mr. Dimple is back for the barest of moments before Topher stands and helps me to my feet. "Let's get you somewhere more comfortable."

My shoulders sagging, I do as he says, following him to the kitchen where he sits me in one of the four wooden chairs. At first, I just stare out at the ocean. None of this would have happened if I'd just followed my first instinct and trekked wherever the beach may have led me.

As Topher rummages in the cabinets for something and tinkers with some mugs, I spot a stack of books on the table. With my side eye, I read the titles. *Ice Skating for Beginners. San Diego's Parade of Lights and Other Holiday Traditions. Best Hiking Trails in California.*

"You sure take your vacations seriously with all this research."

"What? Oh." He returns to the table and slides a cup of something in front of me. Tiny wisps of steam rise from inside. "Here."

The liquid inside is thin and yellow and it smells kind of like grass—though it's honestly difficult to smell anything at all. "What is it?"

"Green tea."

"Didn't have any hot chocolate, huh?" I attempt a grin but it feels crooked somehow.

He frowns in return. "Green tea is good for inflammation and pain, which I'm sure you're experiencing."

Is this man a walking encyclopedia of knowledge? If so, he's a very thoughtful one—and rather adorkable too. "Oh. Well, thank you, then."

I release my nose and wait. Thankfully, it seems the bleeding is done, although my nose feels like someone punched me. "I look awful, don't I?"

A tight expression crosses his face and he glances away from me. "You look fine."

Fine. Just what every girl wants to hear.

Change the subject, change the subject. "So, which of the trails in San Diego is the best so far?"

"Trails?"

I tap the bottom book. "You're reading about hiking trails. I just assumed you had tried some out. Or have you not read this one yet?"

"I finished it a few days ago."

Taking the mug of tea in hand, I blow across the liquid. "And?"

"And … what?"

I laugh. Surely he's not this obtuse. "Which one is the best? Or which are you going to try first?"

"Oh." He lifts his own mug and takes a sip. "I wasn't planning to try any. Well, maybe."

"Why would you take the time to read that whole book if you weren't interested in hiking?"

He brushes at the book cover and shrugs. "I'm interested in gaining knowledge about anything and everything." Then he looks at me again, and his lips flatten. Almost like he's considering me, considering what to say. "I told you I was forced to come here."

"And oh, the agony it must be." I kick him gently in the shin so he knows I'm teasing. "Okay, I'll bite. Why were you forced?"

"Let's just say that I'm an … assistant manager at a … large organization of sorts. The stress was getting to me and one of my bosses—who just so happens to be my mother—booked this house for a month and forbade me from reading anything work related. She sent Frederick along to keep me company."

"Oh, does he work for the same company?"

"Yes." He scratches his head. "I'm technically his boss, but we've been friends since university."

Ah. That totally explains the authoritative vibes I was getting at the hospital. "I did wonder, based on a few things I overheard on Friday night between the two of you."

He squints at me for a moment and grunts. "Yes, well, he's a very protective friend. Sometimes, a little too protective—and invasive. But nevertheless, I trust the man with my life."

"I feel the same way about my friends." I point to the books again. "Where did these come from then?"

"My sister. She knew I would go nutty without something to do while I was here."

"Well, if you were that stressed, it seems the break might be beneficial." Sounds heavenly, if you ask me.

Topher stands and paces. "You'd think that, but all I can consider is how far behind I'm falling at work. Instead of being able to read and study more about being a good … manager, I'm forced to sit here for the past week reading books about things I'll probably never do and wishing I was home instead."

"Topher, just breathe."

He stops, looks at me, and nods, his earlier stiffness returning. "Right. Sorry. I didn't mean to complain. How are you feeling? Should we be done for today?"

"I'm okay." I tilt my head. "So you really have read all of these books and don't have any plans to do anything you're reading about?"

He shrugs. "Why waste my time doing them when I can spend it learning about a new thing?"

"Because have you really learned it if you haven't experienced it for yourself?" I smile. "You can't become a good manager simply by *reading* about tactics and techniques."

"Of course you can. My father did, and his father before him."

"Okay, but maybe there's a better way." An idea springs forward in my brain. It could be really fun—*if* I can get him to agree to it.

His brow crinkles and he sits again, leaning toward me, elbows on his knees. "I'm listening."

"What if instead of being your personal trainer—which clearly I am ill qualified for—I become your tour guide of sorts? I'll help you loosen up and have some experiences here in San Diego that will make you more relatable to your employees. Believe me, when the boss is more relatable, everyone is happy." I nudge him again with my shoe. "And maybe, just maybe you'll have a little fun while you're at it."

"I don't know …"

"Look, you don't have to commit to anything long-term. We can just take it a day at a time."

He sits back and rubs that sexy chin of his. "You won't allow me to pay you for your services if I don't agree to this, will you?"

I just shrug. Because he's totally right.

Topher sighs. "What exactly did you have in mind?"

"I'm not going to tell you." Before he can protest, I stand. "Just be ready tomorrow. I'll text you a time once I get it figured out. All right?"

"I suppose."

Ooo, yes. This is going to be fun.

four

· · ·

WHY DID I ever think this might be fun?

I'm gripping the railing of a speedboat as it races across the Pacific. Even though I'm not yet wet, I shiver in my swim shorts and pink rash guard top while the breeze whips my long hair back. Very soon, I'll be strapped into a harness and lifted over the waters below, my legs dangling, only held aloft by a flimsy parachute.

Me—the girl who isn't the biggest fan of heights. Yeah, kind of forgot that part when I booked this little excursion. Maybe this was a dumb idea.

But then I glance sideways, where Topher stands beside me in swim trunks and a blue T-shirt, sunglasses covering those dreamy eyes of his, and my stomach settles. I'm doing this for him. And for a paycheck.

But mostly, I really do hope to help him. He wants to be a good manager—that much is evident. And I think, for him, it's about more than being a success. I don't even know exactly what kind of company he manages, but I know he wants to help people.

Otherwise, he wouldn't be here either, because he thinks *he's* doing this for *me*.

And maybe I really *can* help him. The first step to being a good manager—a good *anything*, really—is taking care of yourself so you can care for others. If anything is clear, it's that Topher needs to relax and allow himself to have a good time while he's in San Diego.

I may not have many talents, but I do make it my personal mission to bring cheer and light into the world, one person at a time.

"Nervous?" I shout over the roar of the boat's motor.

He turns his face toward me. "Why would I be nervous? I know everything there is to know about parasailing."

"Except how it feels to be weightless. Or to see the skyline from above and not below." Hmm, okay. Maybe I can get behind parasailing after all. It's not the same thing as flying on an airplane or standing at the top of the Empire State Building, because if we fall, we at least drop into the water. That's not all bad, right?

And I'll bet I could get some amazing photos from up there.

Topher lowers his glasses onto the bridge of his nose and peeks down at me. "You look a little pale yourself. Do you need to sit down?"

"I'm fine. Besides, where would I sit?" I glance around at the rest of the boat, which is fairly small and half taken up with the parasailing equipment. Other than Topher and me, there's just the boat captain, Joe, and a parasailing instructor named Denise, who is eyeing Topher like she's Yogi Bear and he's an unattended picnic.

And though Topher hasn't seemed to notice her attention from across the boat, I wouldn't be surprised if he reciprocated her obvious interest. The woman is blonde and tiny everywhere except the chest-al region, and *she* certainly doesn't have a slightly swollen nose from an exercise incident gone awry. Even though I'm not that tall at five-six, I feel like the Jolly Green Giant next to her—and let's not even talk about my pea pods compared with her pumpkins.

The differences are made all the more obvious thanks to her skimpy bikini top and cut-off jean shorts. Is she freaking made of ice? The cold doesn't seem to bother her, anyway.

Topher sidles closer to me. "Are you sure you're all right?"

"Yes." I flash him what is surely the cheesiest smile ever. "Just a little scared of heights, that's all."

"Then why in the world did you bring me here, of all places?"

"You were reading a book on parasailing, duh. And yeah, I may not love being up high, but I've heard it's healthy to face your fears. It'll add to the experience, right?" Oh goodness, please let me be right. I'm totally making this up as I go along, but what's new?

If his curled lip and furrowed brow are any indication, he doesn't quite believe me either. "You're an enigma, Ms. Smith."

I'm not sure if it's a compliment or not, but I gather my wind-blown hair into one fist and lift my chin. "Thank you. And Ms. Smith makes me feel like a grandma. So if you insist on calling me that, I'm going to call you Old-Man James."

For some reason, my reaction brings out Mr. Dimple again and, man, do I have to restrain myself from popping up onto my tiptoes and placing a kiss right there. But since I don't want to scare the guy on what is our first not-really-a-date, I keep my lips to myself like a good girl.

"All right, then. Lauren."

Once again, my name on his lips is like sweet music and I'm gone. I press my mouth into a straight line to keep from grinning.

After a few more minutes of silence between us, the boat slows to a stop. Denise approaches us with a smile directed at Topher, and it's all I can do to not yell at her that there are no free sandwiches or pudding cups here, and she'd best keep on walking. Ahem.

"Sorry we didn't get much of a chance to chat before the boat took off, but we were on a tight schedule," she says.

They actually were five minutes late to pick us up. Apparently, the people before us had a child who didn't want to cooperate.

"It isn't a problem," Topher says.

Upon hearing his accent for the first time—since I did all the talking when we first boarded—Denise's eyebrows perk up practically into her hairline. Clear desire simmers in her eyes like lava bubbling inside a volcano.

And sue me, but I just can't help it. I take a step closer to Topher, and our hands brush. (ACCIDENTALLY, OF COURSE! Cough, cough.)

My heart sinks just a little when he glances down, widens his stance, and crosses his arms over his chest.

And oh, if Denise doesn't looooove that. I can all but hear the cackling in her head as she rubs her hands together with glee—does she even realize she's doing that? "Will the two of you be riding together … or separate?" Her voice goes all sultry with hope at the last word.

I'll bet she'd just love to get me up in the sky all by my lonesome so she can hit on Topher down below. And honestly? It makes me ill just thinking about it.

"Together!" I shout the word like I'm a jury foreman delivering a guilty verdict, an umpire declaring a strike, a—well, you get the picture.

Once again, I can see I've surprised Topher, but he recovers quickly and nods. "Together."

Denise's bottom lip protrudes a bit and I want to pump my fist in her face like a sore winner. But I manage to stay ultra mature and ask, "What do you need us to do?"

That's right, Denise. US. As in, NOT you and Topher.

Okay. Maybe not ULTRA mature.

I'm not sure why my subconscious is so possessive of him, although likely it has something to do with the ringing memory of my friends' comments in my ears when they found out about my little arrangement with Topher.

"The whole thing reminds me of a book I just read. How romantic." One guess who said that. (It was Evie. Anything book-related is always Evie.)

"Mixing business and pleasure can be rewarding sometimes—especially if he's a good kisser." That was Kayla, who was Josh's dating coach for a time before they crossed the line into more. Clearly it worked out for her.

I wonder if Topher is a good kisser …

Uh, anyway. Alexis's comment—*"Generally, I believe men are pigs, but at least he's hot."*—made me LOL the most. But she's not wrong about Topher's sexiness.

"He seems like a nice, genuine guy." Of course that's what Shelby would focus on … but she's *also* not wrong.

Even though there's something kind of stand-offish about Topher, I'm living for those little smiles. He doesn't give them out that often, which makes me feel like I just got paid when I can produce one.

Right now though, he's not smiling—just watching Denise like he's not entirely sure what to make of her. But come on. He *has* to know the effect he (and that accent) has on women.

Speaking of women, Denise ignores my question and taps her chin. "You know, that shirt you're wearing is going to chafe when you're riding in the harness." And with all the subtlety of a rock flying into a window, Denise trails her finger along the collar of Topher's shirt. "Don't worry, I have just the thing."

Then she turns toward one of the seats lining the edge of the boat and lifts the cushion, pulling out a long-sleeved men's shirt that looks like it should fit Topher. She holds it up by the sleeves and gives it a little shake (along with her booty, which unfortunately, is very tight). "This is one of my brother's quick-dry shirts." She points at Joe, who is smacking gum and listening to some Shakira song on the radio. "But he won't mind you borrowing it. Don't worry, it's clean."

"A little chafing doesn't bother me," he says.

Girlfriend clearly doesn't get the hint, because she shoves the shirt into Topher's hands. "Once you're changed, we'll get going with your ride." A pause. "We'll wait."

Oh, she's goooooood. Before I can shout, "I see right through you," Topher shrugs, tosses his sunglasses onto a seat, and peels off his T-shirt.

My mouth betrays me and releases a squeak at the sight of his sculpted bare chest.

I was one thousand percent correct in calling him SuperThor before. His well-shaped pectoral muscles are covered with dark trimmed hair. I seriously have to squeeze my hands into fists to keep them at my side— and I'm not normally a chest-hair kind of girl.

But that's not the only eye candy, not when his abs are wanting to steal the show. The ridges of his stomach are sleek and defined, his obliques sweeping inward and showing off a slim waist where his board shorts ride low.

Despite the chill in the air, it's kind of making me hot all over. Ack. What's wrong with me? I mean, it's not like I've never seen a shirtless man before. I work at a gym, for goodness' sake.

Before I can blink, Topher's got the quick-dry shirt on.

I avert my eyes so he doesn't see me staring. Denise, however, has no such compunction because she's literally rubbing her fingers along her bottom lip. She's a vampire who has spotted her next meal.

"So," I say at an obnoxiously loud volume.

Denise startles and drops her hand, blinking several times in succession before barking out a quick laugh. "So … right. Let's get you love birds up in the sky!"

"Love birds?" Topher squints, then glances between Denise and me. "Oh, we're not together like that."

Never have six words spoken in tandem had the power to crush my spirit more than those. Dang it. I've got it bad and I've only seen the guy a grand total of three times. "Right. We're just …"

Friends? Client and tour guide? Rescuer and rescuee?

"Oh! I just assumed." Denise's teeth are an annoyingly bright white as she grins up at him. "Let's get you strapped in first, all right?"

"Sure." He follows her to the harnesses and I have to look away so they won't see me grinding my teeth at the sight of her running her stupid fingers all over him, taking every opportunity to touch him that she can as she gets him hooked up.

But why am I so upset? *"Oh, we're not together like that."* Obviously, I have no claim on him.

Although, I have to admit I've never felt this burning gravitational pull toward a man so quickly before. And it's not just because he looks like Henry Cavill and Chris

Hemsworth had a baby—there's something deeper there, some mystery that I find myself wanting to tease out, discover.

It's not like he lives here, though. I don't even know how long he's in town. What's the point of delving into the mystery when I may never even reach the end of the book before he leaves?

"Your turn, Lauren."

Denise's tone is as slick as watery syrup on pancakes. I force a smile and turn, my stomach finally remembering what I'm about to do. It clenches and loosens again, and I'm almost afraid my breakfast is going to make an appearance all over the deck of this boat.

But I'm the tour guide. I can't allow Topher to go up there by himself. He'd probably just spout facts at the wind the whole time and not remember to enjoy himself.

"Coming." I make my way over to the harnesses, where Denise cinches mine down so hard I can hardly breathe.

"Oops," she giggles. "Sorry. I set it at the tightness I'd normally need, but I'll let it out a bit for you."

If I wasn't so afraid I was going to barf, I'd try to kill the woman with kindness—that's my typical MO. As it is, all I do is close my eyes and nod.

Clanks, cranks, and whirs reverberate through the air.

"You guys ready?"

I wanna smack the pep right out of Denise's voice.

Not looking, I manage a thumbs-up—and we start to ascend.

"Why are you closing your eyes?"

"So I don't ruin our first parasailing experience with retching of any sort." Oh gross, I did NOT just say that. "Sorry. My stomach just doesn't feel great."

"Hmm." Topher doesn't say anything else for a bit as we get higher and higher into the sky. "Did you know a lot of people confuse parasailing with paragliding? Paragliding is when you're sort of free flying with a glider wing. There's no boat underneath. The directionality of the glider is all reliant upon the pilot."

I can't help it—I laugh and peek at Topher, shaking my head. "I knew you'd do this."

"Do what?" He tilts his head. "Try to distract you from your tumultuous stomach?"

And if I wasn't already flying high, I'd be doing so now, because his thoughtfulness is everything.

I turn my head—and gasp.

Oh, wow. I was wrong. This … this is everything. It's gorgeous up here. The coast and the boat are so tiny. The world has fallen away and it's just me and Topher and the sky. And suddenly, I don't know why I was worried.

The things that seemed large and important just … aren't.

I throw my arms wide and whoop. "This is amazing! Beautiful!"

Topher is quiet in response, but when I look over, he's watching me. I'm desperate to know what's going on in his mind. My cheeks feel warm despite the cold air that should be turning me into a female version of Frosty the Snowman. "What?"

"Nothing." But as he gazes across the ocean, brow furrowed as if he's deep in concentration, Topher nods. "You're right. Amazing. Beautiful."

And I know it's not one of those cheesy romance movie lines where he was looking at me when he said it, but a shiver courses through me all the same.

five

. . .

TWO FEET ON THE GROUND, gliding along, and wearing cute clothing to boot—ice skating is where it's at, my friends.

"I wasn't aware that you could ice skate in San Diego." Topher eyes the beachfront rink with a mixture of curiosity and awe.

"Your sister must have known or she wouldn't have sent you with the book about it, would she?" I smile. "And actually, I didn't know either until Shelby here steered me in the right direction."

I put my arm around my friend, who is looking adorable as ever in a pair of jeans, a soft pink sweater, and a white knit beanie.

Frederick seems to think so too. After I returned Topher safe and sound yesterday afternoon from parasailing, old Freddy boy lectured us for disappearing without inviting him along. (As far as I can tell, he's spending his own vacation lounging around and waiting for Topher to make plans, which is kind of weird if you ask me.)

So I suggested he and Shelby join us today. His eyes lit up at the mention of my friend. And, given her cheek-blushing reaction when I told Shelby as much, it seems poor Eric's got some competition. Either that, or she really doesn't know what a catch she is.

Now all four of us are standing at the edge of the ice rink, our rented skates tied and slung over our shoulders as we scout for a bench. The sun is hanging out just above the horizon line, and even though it's a Thursday evening, the place is hopping. Behind us, the gorgeous Hotel Del Coronado looms, its historic presence always a comfort—reminding me that even though new things come into this world, there are some things that don't change.

Some things that remain.

Shelby shrugs at my comment. "I grew up coming to Skating by the Sea with my family." She's got a whole host of brothers and one sister, all of whom still live in town along with her dad and stepmom.

Once again, a tiny twinge of jealousy takes over. I shove it away. "I can't wait to try it! I haven't ice-skated since …" Oh wait, talking about THAT certainly isn't going to keep the jealousy at bay. "Well, never mind all that. Let's get these skates on and get out there."

Scanning the area, I locate a nearby bench and haul booty toward it. Topher and the others are hot on my heels when I swoop in and claim it. He lowers himself next to me and I can't help but inhale the scent of his cologne. Again. I know, I know, but the stuff is intoxicating. I have half contemplated going to the department store and sniffing colognes like a weirdo until I can find the exact one he wears. I'm not sure what I'd do at that point—definitely not buy a small bottle for my own.

Don't judge. I said HALF contemplated. Which means I'd never actually do it.

Probably.

Besides, given the house he's staying in and the clothing he's wearing—a black Burberry coat that's doing him all sorts of favors—I'd say a tiny bottle of his cologne probably costs more than I make in a month.

I toe off my flats and pull a pair of socks from the pocket of my purple jacket. Leaning down, I slip a sock on my right foot. "Is it cold where ya'll live?"

Frederick, who is sitting on the other side of Topher, stiffens and lifts an eyebrow in his friend's direction. Topher ignores his look and gives a quick nod. "Sometimes."

"Where *do* you guys live?" Shelby asks as she stands on her skates, not even a little wobbly. "I don't think I heard that part."

Frederick pushes off the bench and stands like a pro as well. "A small island in Europe."

Almost the same exact answer Topher gave. What's up with that?

I sit upright before my second foot is in its skate. "Are you both trying to be all mysterious or something?" I crack a smile to show I'm teasing, but the way Frederick throws his arms over his chest and Topher's lips tighten into a straight line shows I've hit some sort of nerve.

But I must have imagined it, because Topher just shakes his head. "No mystery. You've just probably never heard of it. Kentonia."

He's definitely right. "Nope, I would not be able to find that on a map at all." With my final skate on and tied, I stand, nearly pitching forward when the front of it digs into the grass underneath my feet.

"Careful, Tiger." Topher stands like it's no big deal—which, to be clear, is exactly correct. It shouldn't be a big deal.

But this guy … he just has a way of throwing me off balance.

I flip my hair over my shoulder and stick my tongue out at him. "Just watch yourself, SuperThor. I used to be really good at ice skating. So there."

"Tiger? SuperThor?" Frederick pipes up.

Oh, right. I kind of almost forgot that he and Shelby were here. Oops. "Wouldn't you like to know?" Grinning—and praying that any flush in my cheeks can be attributed to the chilly air—I pop my arm through Topher's. "Let's go."

He glances down at me, a bit of surprise rimming the edges. I halfway expect him to extricate himself from my grasp, but he merely says, "Lead the way."

Together we hobble toward the small entrance of the rink. He drops my arm and ushers me forward. *Please don't let me fall.* This guy already must think I'm a train wreck. I don't need to confirm it one more time.

I step onto the ice and find my bearings fairly quickly. Without thinking, I hold out my hand—as if this big hulk of a man needs my assistance. But now that

I think of it, he kind of looks a bit uncertain. One of his hands rubs circles into the palm of the other.

"Wait." I cock my head. "You have ice skated before, right?"

"Once, maybe twice. But I was much younger." His eyes scan the crowd. Maybe he's assessing how they're moving.

I glance behind him, expecting Shelby and Frederick to be waiting, but it appears they've used a different entrance and are already on the ice. Shelby is a graceful swan and Freddy isn't doing so bad himself, keeping up with her and laughing—although he keeps glancing back at us like it's his job to make sure Topher is safe at all times.

I clear my throat. "Well, are you coming or do I need to carry you onto the ice?"

"Now that, I'd like to see." The much-anticipated Mr. Dimple finally arrives to the party and it has me doing an internal fist bump with … uh, myself, I guess.

Gliding toward him, I stop at the edge of the ice and waggle my eyebrows. "I'm game if you are."

His lips are twitching. "You're something else, aren't you?" Then he takes one more step and we're skate to skate. Maybe he's trying to intimidate me as he glances down—and it's true that I definitely can't breathe.

I should back down. Just step away and let him come onto the ice on his own terms. But when has Lauren Everly "Smith" ever done what she should do? (The answer is never. NEVER! Muahahaha!)

Which is why I fling my arms around his middle and use my legs to attempt to lift him.

It's also why we end up sprawled on the ice—this time with Topher on top of me.

He looks down, blinking, likely in shock. If we were in a rom-com movie, there would be a flash of something in his eyes as he lifts his hand and brushes my hair out of my face, then lowers his gaze to my lips. Then he would kiss the heck outta me right here and now.

But before I know it—because, hi, this is reality and not some made-up fictional world—he's scrambling upright, pulling me to a sitting position quickly before a small child can run me over.

Topher puts his hand protectively around my back. "Are you all right?"

"Just embarrassed. Sorry. I don't know what I was thinking."

But I know the answer. I wasn't.

"That's the problem with you, Lauren. You don't think. You just do. And that failure to plan is going to hurt you one of these days." Ugh, why is my mother's voice in my head again? GET OUT! GET. OUT! I don't care what she thinks. I'd rather live my life impulsively than plan so much I suck the joy out of everything.

"You know," he says, his head tilted. "We've got to stop meeting like this." Then, without warning, Topher laughs—and even though it's quick and rough, the sound is simply glorious. It's like liquid gold spilling out onto a dry and broken earth. I just want to sit here and marvel in it all night long.

But my rear end is starting to get seriously soaked on this ice.

Withholding my smile, I stand, holding my hands to help him up. "I'm glad one of us finds this so amusing."

He stands without assistance—which is probably safer for all involved, really. His expression goes slack. "I hope I haven't offended you."

"Not at all. Being able to laugh at yourself is one of the best qualities a person can have, in my opinion." And one I've been sure to cultivate since being out of the social media spotlight that Danny and my mother created for me.

"I like that a lot." Topher furrows his brow as he starts to move on the ice—a bit wobbly at first, then more sure. "I'm not very good at it myself."

"There's always room for improvement." I follow him cautiously, but then the feeling of the ice beneath my skates becomes more familiar. By now, the sun has fully disappeared and the twinkle lights strung over the rink have flipped on. The whole place is surrounded by palm trees, and just beyond the rink, the sand and rocky beach of Coronado Island stand guard.

I sigh in contentment, allowing my muscles to relax. "This is a nice ending to my crazy day."

He adjusts the collar of his jacket. "What did you do?"

"I spent my time in the company of thirty kinder-gartners."

"Why on earth would anyone choose to do that?"

I bark out a laugh. "One day a week, I work as Shelby's teacher's aide. She got me the job at the beginning of the school year when I was looking for something new."

"I thought you worked at a gym? Although given your personal training skills, I'm not sure I believe that one." The quirk of his attractive mouth means he's teasing me.

"I warned you about my experience level beforehand." After sticking out my tongue at him, I hold out my hands to steady myself as we round the bend. "But I've been teaching both cycling and basic strength training classes for years now. I just do the teacher's thing on the side. And now I'm a barista too at the coffee shop where Kayla and her husband work."

"I see." He puts his hands behind his back as he skates almost effortlessly, dodging an older couple going about half our speed. Is it terrible that I hoped he'd be just a little bit bad at this? It would go toward proving my point that he can't be good at something or experience it just by reading about it. "Did you always want to be an instructor of some sort?"

"Not really. I just sort of fell into it."

"It must be nice to have a choice in your profession."

For a moment, we're separated as Frederick skates quickly between us, laughing in that way dudes have when they're roasting each other. Shelby follows, apologizing as she goes.

"Looks like they're hitting it off." Then I turn back to Topher, pursing my lips as I consider him. "So you don't have a choice?"

He sneaks a glance at me, then turns back to the ice, which has gotten fairly crowded at this point. "I'm expected to go into the family business."

Oh, yeah. "Your mom's your boss, right?"

"Something like that."

"And what does your company do, exactly?"

He coughs and then, without warning, stops at one of the exits. "I'm getting hungry. How about you?"

I try to halt as quickly, but before I can fall, he grabs one of my hands and pulls me against him. "Um, thanks." And I'm in heaven for zero-point-two seconds before he releases me.

"No worries. So? Food?"

It's nearing dinnertime and my stomach chooses that moment to give a growl. "I could eat. Should we get Frederick and Shelby?" I scan the ice for them, but can't locate them in the bustling crowd.

"They can find us."

"All right."

We step off the ice and sit to unlace our skates. Once I have my shoes back on, I blow into my hands, which are ice cubes at this point.

"You cold?"

"Oh, it's not a big deal. I just didn't think to bring gloves." Who needs those in Southern California?

But apparently, Topher came prepared, because he produces a pair of woven gloves from his pocket and holds them out to me. "I'm sure they're too big, but here. Wear these."

"Oh, I couldn't." *And by that I mean, YES! GIMME GIMME!*

He shifts his body sideways so our knees press against each other. Then he takes one of my hands in his. "I insist."

One finger at a time, he tugs on the glove. The whole

thing seems to happen in slow motion, and all I can do is stare at him in the dim light. His eyes are on my hands, his focus intent. Does he give this much care and attention to everything he does?

If so, the woman who ends up with him is going to be the luckiest person on the planet.

When he's done, our gazes connect again and I swallow against the dryness in my throat. "Thanks." Then, because I can't stand the static tension in the air—which I know I'm probably imagining—I hold up my hands and let the excess glove material flop at the end of my fingers. "They fit great."

Smiling, he stands and shoves his hands into his pockets. "Come on, Tiger. Let's get you fed."

"I never turn down a chance to eat." Standing, I follow him toward a rink-side lounge offering cocktails and tapas.

After chatting with the hostess, we grab a seat on a plush bench with enough room for Frederick and Shelby, whom I text with our location. In front of us, a fire pit puts off a wonderful heat, its flames crackling. I order a peppermint schnapps cocktail for Shelby plus a hot chocolate with extra whipped cream for myself—to which Topher lifts an eyebrow before ordering a cranberry mule. We also ask for an array of appetizers that should suit everyone. Large festive garland strung with red and gold ornaments and oversized bows hangs along the clear wall that separates us from the rink. From somewhere above us, Bing Crosby sings "White Christmas."

The waitress delivers a basket of bread before darting off to help other customers.

"You were quite the natural out there despite not having skated much," I say.

"I could say the same about you." Reaching forward, he snags a piece of crusty bread, breaks it in two, and hands me the other half. "Earlier, you said something about not having ice skated since … something. You didn't finish your thought."

"You caught that, did you?"

"I know I seem like I have my head in my books all day long, but I can be observant now and again."

I shoulder bump him, smiling. "I see that."

He stops, bread suspended midair on its way to his mouth, and looks at me, his brow a picture of confusion. That's twice now tonight that he has seemed surprised by my casual touch. But why?

Maybe he thinks I'm flirting with him. Maybe I am. Maybe he doesn't like it.

And maaaaaaybe I should stop overthinking things and just answer his question.

I plow on. "Yeah, so what I was going to say is that I haven't skated since I was in high school. My family moved to New York City when I was twelve, and ice skated a few times at Rockefeller Center. You know, where there's that ginormous Christmas tree?"

He nods, chewing his bread thoughtfully, his eyes warmer than I have seen them before.

"Anyway, it was so much fun that we said we'd make it a tradition. And we did. Until …"

Topher swallows. "Until what?"

How much do I tell him? But what harm is there in revealing everything? I've never been someone to hold myself back from others—authenticity is something I crave. The only way to get it is to be vulnerable, and I can do that, one on one. It's only when it becomes part of public consumption that things get muddied and you can't tell the difference between what's real and what's for show.

"We actually moved from Texas after my mom and stepdad—my sister's father—got divorced. Mom had always dreamed of being an interior decorator, and she had this friend who offered her an amazing opportunity in Manhattan."

The waitress delivers our drinks and we thank her. I pick up mine and sip. Mmm. I'll never tire of hot chocolate as long as I live.

"That's a long way to move. How old were you?"

"Not gonna lie, it was hard. But I knew my mom needed it, you know? A fresh start. First, my dad died when I was a baby and she was a single mom for years until my stepdad, Randall, came into the picture. Despite that, she'd always been such a wonderful, involved mother. Think the PTA mom, the leader of the Girl Scout group, the kind of mom who never missed a single one of my gymnastics competitions." My fingers press into the warmth of my mug. "If only I knew then what I do now …"

"And what's that?"

"I'm getting there." I take a deep breath, the chill in the air moving through my nose to my core. "So after working a few years in New York, my mom landed a job with a high-profile client—the actress, Larissa Lorraine." Studying Topher, I look for signs of recognition, but he just frowns as if he knows where this is going. But how can he? "Well, Larissa loved my mom's work and spread the word. Seemingly overnight, my mom was a huge success. Which would have been wonderful if ..."

I set my drink back on the table and sigh.

Topher doesn't push me. He just waits, his eyes not leaving mine.

Finally, I get the words to say more. "Success changed her. When I was sixteen, she missed my state gymnastics tournament, and she didn't even apologize. She just said, 'Sometimes we have to make hard choices in pursuit of our dreams.'" My hands make fists inside the gloves Topher lent me and I pop them against my kneecaps. "I determined then and there that if dreams mean I have to put something above the people I love, then I'd rather not have them. Nothing grandiose, anyway. I'm happy just being me and living the life of my choosing."

"I can understand that." Topher rubs his chin with his fingers. "And I admire it. I ... admire you."

"You shouldn't." Whew, it's suddenly suuuuuuper warm. I peel off his gloves and place them on the seat between us, shaking my head with fervor. "I'm the girl who runs away when things get too hard."

"What do you mean?"

He might as well know it all. Much as I'd like to have his admiration, I can't have him thinking false thoughts about me. "I haven't seen my mom or sister in five years. Something ... happened. Something that made me realize that we had different values—specifically, my mom. See, she's become really famous. Huge on social media. Even has her own television show now. And I just couldn't stand it anymore, you know? How she'd put on one face at home and another out in front of the world to see. When you're famous like that, it's so easy to lose yourself, to care more what the world at large thinks of you—and your image—than what those closest to you think."

Topher is quiet, but I swear his thoughts are shouting at me.

I just wish I knew what they were saying.

But something inside pushes me to finish my story. "Topher, success and fame ruined my family. And after …" Okay, maybe I don't need to go into the whole Danny-slash-accident thing. Not right now. "Well, I left to preserve what little bit of myself I had left. Now, other than random recipe searches and GPS, I stay off the Internet altogether. I don't even let my friends post my photo on social media or have accounts myself. How pathetic is that?"

He shifts in his seat and drapes his arm along the back of the bench. Somehow, I feel his phantom touch.

"I don't think it's pathetic. But why don't you allow it? Are you afraid your family will find you before you're ready to see them again?"

"Not my family, but maybe some of my mother's crazy fans or the media who will make a big deal out of locating the daughter Margaret Everly never talks about anymore." There have been lots of theories about what happened to me after the accident, because apparently people have nothing better to do than make up stories about a stranger whose life they know nothing about. "I love the quiet little life I've built here, and I don't ever want that to change."

I shake off the familiar frustration edging in. "As for my mom and sister, they know I'm in California. And I do still text my sis sometimes, just to check in. Say happy birthday. That kind of thing. But she never says much in reply. And I don't blame her." I sigh. "She was away at college when I left and doesn't understand what happened. At first she tried to convince me to come back. But I couldn't, so I found it easier to just stop talking altogether for a while. And I haven't even tried talking to my mom." I lift my left leg onto the bench sideways, so I'm sitting fully facing him.

"That's rough. I'm sorry."

"It is what it is."

We fall into silence, and suddenly I snap out of it. Whoa. Things got serious fast. I take my drink in hand again and thrust on a wide grin. "Let's toast, okay?"

After a moment, he lifts his drink and clinks it against my own. "What are we toasting?"

"To … new adventures. And getting back up when we've been knocked down."

That earns me another visit from my favorite dimple. "We are certainly gaining lots of experience in that arena, aren't we?"

"We certainly are." I imitate his accent as I say this, inhaling a sip of chocolate and smiling over the rim of my mug at his returned laughter.

six

FRIENDS DON'T LET friends kidnap other friends.

Or, at the very least, they try to talk them out of it.

"Are you sure about this, Kay?" I whisper, tugging on the back of Kayla's silver beaded dress. "You're going to give poor Evie a heart attack."

"Yeah, and what's a bachelorette party without a trip to the ER?" Rolling her eyes, Alexis leans against the side of Evie's office building, her now-purple hair done in a messy ponytail down her back.

"Shhh, all of you." Her four-inch stilettos placed firmly on the ground, Kayla leans forward and glances around the corner again. "I think she's coming."

We look utterly ridiculous, all dressed to the nines in cocktail dresses on a Friday at five-thirty—and freezing, might I add—and waiting in the gravel parking lot outside Evermore Publishers.

Behind me, Shelby is hopping up and down in her

pale pink dress, arms folded over her chest to try to stay warm. "She's going to hate us."

"She'll love it," Kayla hisses.

Alexis snorts and that sets me to giggling. I love these women.

"Okay, there she is. Almost here." We wait a few more seconds. "On three," Kayla directs. "One, two—"

"Three!" We all scream and rush from our hiding place as gracefully as we can in heels and short skirts—which, as it turns out, is not all that gracefully, because we stumble and bump into one another.

Eyes wide, Evie pulls up short, one hand on her heart, the other tossed across Connor's chest like a driver trying to protect her car passenger from smacking the dashboard during a hurried stop.

She blinks. "What in the name of Pemberley is going on here?"

"Language." Beside her, Connor laughs. "It's called a bachelorette party, Webster."

Her brown hair, which she recently chopped to her shoulders, swings as she squints at her fiancé. "You knew about this?"

He stoops to kiss her, then hands her his messenger bag. "Your dress and flats are in here. I know how much you hate heels."

"You …" She does her best impression of Kayla's glare, but it just doesn't have quite the same effect. "You're supposed to be on my side, Almost Husband."

Gah, they are too cute for words. I still remember Evie coming home after the earthquake last February, when she was stuck in her office building overnight with Connor Bryant, the supposed ladies' man who had never shown a lick of interest in her before. She'd been so determined not to like him, and look at her now. She's clinging to his neck and acting for all intents and purposes like we don't exist.

Maybe, in her mind, we don't.

"Don't worry, Almost Wife." Connor waggles his eyebrows. "They said they'd take good care of you."

"Let's go." Alexis marches forward and tugs Evie away from Connor. "I'm freezing my rear off over here."

"Yeah, come on, Evs." Kayla flings her arm around her best friend. "Don't you trust us?"

"I trust the rest of them." Evie smiles. "Not sure about you, though."

Laughing, Shelby and I link arms and join the group. "She's got you there, Kay." But Kayla doesn't know what we have in store for *her* tonight. It's going to be fabulous just seeing her face.

The gaggle of us walk through the parking lot toward the limo we rented for the night. At the sight of it, Evie gets teary-eyed. "You guys. This is too much. Thank you."

"Don't thank us just yet." Alexis climbs inside—and emerges with a life-size cardboard cutout. "And for the record, this was not my idea."

Connor cough-laughs. "Is that … me?"

We all lose it. I couldn't believe it when Kayla came over three nights ago with an arm filled with crafting supplies. She tossed one of Connor's suits at us, and instructed us to find a photo of his face, blow it up to life-size proportions, cut it out, and glue it on the cardboard figure she was about to create.

"Of course it's you." Kayla elbows the cardboard figure in the side, a wicked grin on her face. "Did you think I wanted to borrow your clothes so I could play dress-up?"

Evie's nostalgic tears have turned to a flood of laughing ones. "Just … why?"

"Because you used to have a cardboard cutout of Mr. Darcy—or so you tell me—and I thought you should have the real deal for your bachelorette party."

We all release a chorus of awwwws.

"And that's my cue to leave." Connor slips Evie another kiss, then walks up to the cardboard figure and salutes. "Be on your best behavior, you handsome devil, you."

We're all laughing as he walks away, then pile into the nice, warm limo.

Where Kayla promptly screeches. "What is *that*?"

Alexis has slid into the back-facing seat, where yet another cardboard creation sits beside her. "Oh, this guy?" She points with her thumb. "Didn't we tell you Josh was coming along for the ride?"

Kayla's mouth has fallen. Evie's lips twitch as she digs through the bag Connor brought.

Shelby pulls two sashes and two tiaras from behind a seat. "Ta-da! This isn't just Evie's bachelorette party."

"It's yours too, Kay," I say. "You got married before we could throw you one, so we figured why not combine them?"

"But …" Crouching, she approaches fake-Josh and

pokes him in the face. "He doesn't look quite right without his glasses."

"Oh, yeah." I rummage in my purse and pull out my drugstore purchase—a pair of thick black readers that resemble Josh's glasses to a fairly close degree. Tugging off the little price tag, I toss them and a roll of masking tape to Alexis, who affixes them to cardboard-Josh's face. "There you go."

Evie's across the limo attempting to get undressed and redressed without showing any skin. The woman is hilariously modest sometimes. But right now, she pauses, her red dress pulled just over her boobs while her blouse is still on underneath. "So what exactly are we doing tonight?"

I bust out several champagne flutes, start filling them, and pass them around. "You know, the usual. Dinner, drinks, dessert—and a good, old-fashioned scavenger hunt."

"Which involves what?"

"You'll see." She might jump out of the vehicle now if I tell her she has to approach complete strangers and perform a variety of silly tasks—from finding a guy named Connor to letting a random person give her a fake tattoo on her arm and using a cheesy pickup line on someone.

"You guys are crazy." We all drink some champagne while Evie finishes changing and our driver takes us to our first stop.

When we arrive, we climb from the vehicle in front of a popular upscale Mexican food restaurant down-town. Tonight the sky is cloudy, but thankfully no rain is in the forecast. The old-timey wrought-iron lampposts that line the streets are lit up, and the awnings of various restaurants and shops extend over the outdoor eating areas warmed by heaters.

Just like most Friday nights, there are people everywhere—coming, going, and sitting. I love the electricity of thousands of people in one place. It's one thing I miss about New York City, though I get to experience it on a smaller scale here as well.

Evie claps her hands together. "Aw, you guys. This is one of the first restaurants I went to with Connor. It's my favorite."

"We know." I hip bump her. "The whole night isn't meant to embarrass you."

"Just some parts of it." Alexis emerges from the vehicle with Cardboard Connor in tow. Shelby follows with Cardboard Josh, an apologetic look on her face.

Evie looks horrified. "What do you mean?"

Kayla is laughing. "I almost forgot—we have to bring the men with us everywhere we go tonight." She side-eyes Shelby. "Hey, watch where you're touching my man."

Shelby glances down and realizes her hands are placed between the cutout's legs—which, to be fair, is probably the easiest place to carry a giant cardboard dude. Gasping, the poor thing turns red and drops Fake Josh right on his face. "I'm so sorry, Kayla."

"I was just kidding." Kayla cackles and squats to pick up her "husband."

"Maybe this isn't such a great idea," Evie says.

I take Connor from Alexis and shake him back and

forth in front of Evs. "Oh, come on, babe." I lower my voice. "Give me a smooch."

That has her laughing and taking the six-foot-something monstrosity from me. "This is going to be utterly mortifying."

"Hold your head high, girl." Chin up, Kayla and her fake hubby stroll past us and through the restaurant's front door. Evie scurries to follow.

I link arms with Alexis and Shelby. "Well, ladies. Maybe someday that will be us."

"Maybe sooner for some of us than others," Shelby teases. "You and Topher looked pretty cozy when Frederick and I finally found you last night."

We breeze through the restaurant's front door, met with the delicious smell of melted cheese and salsa. The hostess is already seating Kayla and Evie—looking appropriately horrified at their choice of "companions" —so we head in that direction.

"He is pretty great." I heave a contented sigh. "We're going Christmas tree shopping tomorrow night because he and Frederick are going to be here right up until Christmas and they don't have a tree. Can you believe that?"

"That two men on vacation don't have a Christmas tree? Yes, I can," Alexis says dryly. "Should you really be getting this attached, though? Doesn't he live really far away?"

"Way to be a buzzkill, Lexi Lou." I stick my tongue out at her. "And yes, he does. Somewhere near England." I purposefully haven't told my friends the name of Topher's country. Knowing them, they'd do a

Google search or run a background check on him and then try to report back to me. Call me crazy, but I'd rather Topher be the one to tell me about himself—*and* his country. Places are much better when seen through the eyes of someone who lives there, after all.

We slide into the booth where Evie and Kayla are already looking at menus.

"I just don't want to see you get hurt," Alexis sputters. "Like I always say—"

"Men are pigs," the rest of us join in. Then we're all laughing. All of us but Alexis.

"What? They are. Take this guy at work, Dax. He's just so …" Her hands clench her menu and give it a good shake. "Argh. He's Mr. Popular around the office, though I can't fathom why except that he's my boss's nephew—which is how he keeps stealing the promotions. It's despicable." She shoves her nose into her menu.

The rest of us raise eyebrows at each other. Alexis is usually pretty tight-lipped about her job, so this is the first we've heard of this Dax guy.

"Is Dax … cute?" I manage without laughing, though the tremor in my voice probably gives me away.

Slowly, like a stealth ninja, Alexis lowers the menu. The tension is thick as we all wait with bated breath to hear what she says.

Then, just before my lungs nearly fail me, she speaks. "Irrelevant."

Her growled word leaves the rest of us hooting.

"So he *is* cute!"

"Lexi's got a crush! Finally!"

"We need to meet this guy."

Alexis picks up her knife and holds it in front of her face. She looks so hilarious with her lime green dress and purple hair, a scowl marring her otherwise smooth skin. "Not happening, because there is honestly no one on Earth I could be *less* interested in." Setting down the knife, she scans the restaurant. "Now where is our waitress? Looks like I'm gonna need about a thousand drinks tonight."

"You and me both, sister." Kayla hooks a thumb at Cardboard Josh, which has us in fits of laughter once again.

When the waitress comes, she takes our drink order —extra-large margaritas all around—and brings us a basket of chips and salsa. As I take a chip between my teeth, I soak in this moment. I know Kayla is already married, but that's still so new that we haven't felt the full effects yet.

In a week and a half, it'll be Evie's turn.

All of this—it's about to change. While that's wonderful in a way, it's also really hard, a reminder that change is the only constant. And when these ladies—my family—all have their own little families to care for, where will that leave me?

"Lauren." Evie looks at me with concern in her eyes. "Why are you frowning?"

"Me? Oh, no reason." I paste on a smile and peruse the menu some more. "Just didn't see a chimichanga on the menu, and that's my fave."

Shelby leans over and points to a gi-hugic picture of a chimi in the center of the page. "Right here, friend."

I smile. "Yay."

"Uh uh. You aren't fooling any of us." Kayla folds up her menu and grabs a chip. "What's going on with you?"

"She's in love with a dude who's leaving in a few weeks, that's what," Alexis says.

"In love?" Evie's eyebrows lift.

"Isn't that kind of fast? What do you really know about this guy?" Her lips curling, Kayla examines her chip. "At the hospital, he seemed a little shady to me. Like he's hiding something. Besides, he was too quick to help. Too … nice."

"This coming from the woman who married Josh Gregory, the nicest man in the world." Evie rolls her eyes, smiling. Then she refocuses on me. "But seriously. Do you really like him or are you just attracted to him?"

"Yes."

We all chuckle, and I'm temporarily saved by the waitress as she delivers our drinks and takes our food orders. But as soon as she's gone, my friends zero in on me once again.

"I'm not in love." I take a sip of my margarita, and the bite of the lime and tequila feels appropriate.

"But you really like him." Shelby stirs her drink, creating a slow yellowish tornado in her glass.

The wall behind Evie and Kayla suddenly becomes super interesting. I try to make out the shapes, but it's a geometric mess of greens and browns and yellows. Then I tilt my head a bit and find the starting point of the picture—and suddenly, it all makes sense.

Maybe life is like that too.

"I'll be honest. I haven't met a man who makes me feel like Topher in … well, maybe never. But I have no idea how he feels about me, because he's so quiet and seems hesitant to tell me too much about his life."

For a moment, my friends all just sip and crunch on their chips. See? None of them knows what to make of all this either.

I'm not really averse to a relationship, but it has to be with the right guy. I've dated here and there, but nothing serious. And I just have this gut feeling that dating Topher could never be some fling.

I can't take the silence anymore. This is supposed to be a party. "But Alexis is right—he's leaving in two weeks. So even if he liked me back, it doesn't matter anyway."

"I'm calling shenanigans on that one." Kayla taps her lip, and her diamond reflects the light of the candles on our table. "Look, Lauren. You know me. I can't help but give dating advice. I do it for a living now, you know."

I widen my eyes in pretend shock. "You do? I had no idea."

"Ha ha. Who knows? Maybe I'm wrong about him. Maybe he's the greatest guy in the world—besides my Joshy here, of course." Kayla pats Cardboard Josh on the head. "And as Evie and I can attest to, sometimes love finds you when you least expect it."

Evie nods a little too voraciously. She's quite the lightweight, so I have a feeling she's already feeling the effects of her half-downed margarita. "Be cautiously optimistic."

"Lauren, cautious?" Alexis lifts an eyebrow and laughs. "That'll be the day."

It's true—I'm impulsive. Not normally a worrier. I try my best to be the kind of woman open to whatever the universe wants to throw my way. And it's served me well so far.

"You're so right!" With a tad too much excitement (because maybe Evie isn't the only lightweight around here), I fling my arms wide and accidentally smack Cardboard Connor sideways. His hand lands right on Evie's chest.

"Connor, you rogue!" she cries, her voice taking on some sort of Southern accent that only a tipsy Evie can produce. "Not in front of all these people."

And that's it. We. are. dying. The poor waitress brings our food and we're a mess of tears and laughter. No question about it. This night will go down in history as one of the best of my life.

But … there are so many days left to live. So much left to experience. And if I am always letting fear stand in my way, I won't experience any of it. If I never tilt my head, I'll never see the full picture.

Okay, Universe. Do your thing.

seven

...

"I STILL CAN'T BELIEVE you wanted to order this baby online." I lovingly stroke a branch of the Douglas fir Topher and I purchased an hour ago. After carting it home on top of his rented Porsche, we wrangled the eleven-foot beast through his front door. Frederick magically appeared to help us cut a half-inch off the butt of the tree and locate a bucket of water to stand it in. "You would have missed the whole experience."

"You mean the experience where you pretended we were newlyweds?" Topher pops the top off a box that's in the corner of his living room.

"She did what?" Frederick enters the room, a soda in hand. "I'd have paid good money to see that." He chuckles then grows serious as his gaze narrows in on Topher. "You should have let me know you were going so I could tag along."

And once again, there seems to be a weird undercurrent of tension between them for a moment. And that doesn't make sense, because why would Freddy want to come with us? Maybe he's bored. Or maybe they had plans and Topher blew them off, though that doesn't sound like him given what I know so far.

I jump in. "I overheard the manager telling another couple they could have a discount because they were celebrating one month of marriage, so I thought, why not try it?" It had seemed like a good idea at the time—that is, until I plopped my hand inside of Topher's and it felt oh so right.

That wasn't the bad part. It was the way he looked down, confused. Unsure.

As soon as the charade was up, I released him and pretended all was well—despite the thick dryness in my throat.

Frederick pops the top of his soda and takes a sip. I hear the fizzy carbonation give way from where I'm standing. He cocks his head and eyes the box Topher is currently digging through. "What's in there?"

"Just a few decorations." Topher proceeds to pull out lights, tinsel, and more ornaments than I have collected over my lifetime.

I step closer and see most of them are in pristine condition with tags still on. "Did you just buy all of this?"

He shrugs and hands me a smaller box of fat, red ball ornaments. "You said we were going to decorate, so I made my way to a local Christmas shop and asked the owner what I would need. She was most helpful."

I'll bet she was. Probably included her phone number along with half her store. "I think you got fleeced. There's enough decor here for ten trees. You should return some of it."

"Maybe you can find someone to donate it to."

"Oh." That's actually a really great idea. "Well, I know Shelby mentioned there are some families at school doing without a lot this year."

His head lifts and there are these little creases between his brows showcasing his concern. "That sounds like a great plan. Perhaps we could go shopping for some extra toys and other things to stick under the tree as well."

If my heart wasn't already in fits over this man, I'm pretty sure I'd have a straight-up coronary at the sudden tug I feel toward him. "That's really generous."

"Yeah, it is. Maybe you could do some of that *online*." Frederick stares at Topher over the top of his can as he takes another sip. Is he trying to Jedi mind trick him or something? What's his deal?

But Topher stands, a ball of lights in hand. "I rather liked being out among the people today."

"Whoa, whoa, whoa." I hold up my hands in mock surprise. "Did you just admit to enjoying yourself shop-ping?" Most men hate it.

"I concede nothing." But the little smirk makes me want to do a jig.

Setting down my small box of ornaments, I steal the dangling end of lights from him so we can wrap them around the tree together. "I think I'm going to make a better manager out of you yet." I turn to Frederick. "Want to help us decorate?"

"Ah, no. My expertise is best kept to being the

muscle." Raising his can of soda, Frederick heads down the hallway.

"All right, so how do we go about doing this?" Topher asks. "My research only extends to selecting the best tree, not what to do with it once we got it home."

The way he says "home" makes everything in me warm and gooey, like I'm being slowly cooked from the inside out. I know he doesn't mean it the way my stupid heart is taking it, but for just a moment, I wonder what it would be like if this was *our* home—not just his vacation rental in a city that he will probably never visit again.

"Haven't you ever decorated a tree before?" I tease.

"Not really. Our servants always did it for us."

"Ooo, servants. I knew you were rich, but had no idea it was on *that* level."

His cheeks redden. "You have no idea," he mutters. Hmmm. Well, at least it doesn't sound like he's obsessed with wealth, even if he does have workaholic tendencies. "So what's first then?"

I glance around the room and locate a ladder leaning against the fireplace. "We'll need that to string the lights." Dropping the strand, I snag the ladder.

He hustles over. "Here, let me help."

It probably sounds creepy, but I know where he's at in the room because of his cologne. And right now, it's in my space, surrounding me, taking me captive. *I'll be your hostage all day long.*

Stop talking to his cologne, Lauren, you freak.

"I've got it. You might think I'm a klutz, but I'm not usually like that." Then I use my legs to lift and carry the ladder toward the tree, positioning it open without incident.

He approaches, placing a hand on a rung of the ladder. "Now why would I think you're a klutz? Could it be because you're constantly falling all over yourself around me?"

My mouth falls open at his jesting and I give him a light shove. "Must be your charming personality that's affecting me so much. In fact, I should just call you Prince Charming instead of SuperThor."

At that, his face blanches. He straightens and whirls, marching right back to the box of ornaments.

What just happened? I thought we were teasing each other, but clearly I misread the situation. "Topher? Did I do something wrong?"

"Sorry. No. You didn't do anything." Topher frowns and rejoins me, his hands empty. "It's me. Lauren, I …"

And the man looks so darn uncomfortable that I just want to ease his pain. I pick up the lights and place them back into his hands, then run over to my purse. "We need music if we're going to decorate a tree, now don't we?" I navigate to my favorite Christmas playlist and the tune of Mariah Carey's "All I Want for Christmas Is You" fills me with instant peace.

Climbing the ladder, I extend my hand. "Here, give me the end of the lights. Then, you can go stand on the other side of the tree and we can wrap the strand around the trunk together."

Though he continues to frown and brood, Topher hands me the lights and does as I say. To fill the time, I tell him all about the bachelorette party last night—including the cardboard cutouts of Connor and Josh.

"That's ... undignified."

"Eh, what is dignity anyway?" I wave my hand in the air while waiting for him to hand the lights back around. We're making good progress, and this tree is going to look so lovely all lit up in front of the wall of windows. I'll have to suggest we go to the beach once it's dark to see how it looks from there.

If he doesn't kick me out before that, of course.

"It was really fun, and I needed that," I continue. "The holidays are sometimes really hard, being away from my family. But my friends are my family now, and I'm so glad they're here."

"Do you think there's a chance they'd ever move?"

Why is he asking that? And, gah, how have I never thought of that particular scenario before? "I hope not."

"What about you? Would you ever move?" He says it so casually, but there's something in his tone that gives me pause before answering.

"I don't think I'd ever leave San Diego, to be honest." Even if I finally see Mom and Sam again, this is home now.

"Never?"

The single word reverberates through the room. I peek up and his eyes are fixed on mine. He's searching for something, but for the life of me, I have no idea what. "Um, I don't know. Why?"

"No reason." He goes back to focusing on weaving the strand of lights through the tree. "Do you miss your family this time of year especially?"

"Of course. Well, I miss what we used to be. Relaxed, loud. Fun. A few years after we moved, though, my mom became so obsessed with everything looking perfect that she had to take a whole slew of pictures on Christmas morning before we were allowed to touch the presents. Oh, and our Christmas pajamas were no longer appropriate for opening presents—we had to dress up in our Christmas best."

I sigh, remembering how fake those last few years had felt. "What about you?" I peek through the branches and our gazes meet. His is warm and open—the Topher I've seen a few times so far. Maybe that's who he is really, and the stiff version is just a facade. Something in me aches to know. "What's your family like? Do you miss them?"

"I do." He hands me the lights and our fingers brush. Then Topher clears his throat. "Both of my parents are brilliant, and my mum and sister are outgoing and vivacious. You remind me a lot of them, actually."

"Really?"

"Well, I'm not sure they'd fling themselves at total strangers—"

"Hey!" Now I'm laughing.

His chuckle fills the room—and my chest. "But yes. There's a certain authenticity to you all. Now my father, he's a lot more like me. Reserved. Cautious."

"Dignified?" I say with a tease in my voice.

"Quite."

"Then I'll have to remember to give him a huge hug when we first meet."

Too late, I realize what I've said. *Way to stick your foot in it, Lauren.* Ugh. Now Topher knows that I'm not opposed to the idea of meeting his family and may in fact have pictured it despite having only known the man for eight days.

"I'd like to see that." His eyes shine with mirth.

Huh. Okay, so maybe he's not running for the hills just yet.

Maybe he actually likes you too.

Time will tell, I guess. Or I could just do what a very tipsy Kayla told me last night just before she fell asleep on Alexis's bright blue couch—"If all else fails, you grab that man and give him the best darn kiss of his life!"

Um, that's a big fat NEVER GONNA HAPPEN.

We finish wrapping the last bit of lights around the tree and I climb down the ladder, brushing a few pine needles from my sweater to the floor. "Yay! Time for ornaments." Walking to the stack that Topher unboxed, I pick up a box of glass angels. "So is your sister older or younger?"

"Older by two years."

"What's her name?"

He pauses, glances at me before hanging the ornament in his hand with such precision that an army general would be proud. "Chloe."

"That's a pretty name. My sister is Samantha. She's younger by eight years." The flood of guilt and sadness I usually feel when thinking of my sister crashes in. "She was only four when we moved to New York, so she doesn't really remember much about life before. She thinks what we had there was normal. And that's what grieves me the most. There are times I'm not sure I should have left so that I could have shown her there was a better way, you know?"

I held on for years, really. But then there had been Danny and the accident … and I just couldn't take it anymore. I had to leave so I could do my own healing.

"I hope someday she'll forgive me for leaving." I brush away a tear. "I just hope she doesn't hate me."

"I don't think anyone could hate you, love." Topher is standing next to me now, the sleeve of his sweater brushing against mine as he hangs an icicle drop ornament near my angel.

For a moment I just stand there, my heart clipping along like a horse in the Kentucky Derby. He sometimes just says these … things … that both surprise and delight me. And I don't want to read too much into them, but they feel special somehow, like little pearls I want to grab from the sand and tuck away, just for myself.

I glance up to find him already looking at me, and it's one of those moments where the air between us feels hot to the touch, stinging my face and my hands with its intensity. It's all I can do not to turn into his embrace—but he still hasn't really indicated he wants that.

Licking my lips, I finally manage a reply. "Thank you."

He studies me for a moment, then reaches up and touches my face, his thumb giving my cheek the slightest caress. I'm lost in his gaze and he's lost in mine, or so it seems until his hand suddenly drops and he shakes his head. "Sorry, you had an … eyelash there."

"Oh." Is that true—or did we just have a moment and now he's backing away?

Before I can think too much about that whatever-it-was between us, an 'N Sync Christmas song comes on the radio.

And then, the most glorious thing happens.

Topher turns back to the tree and starts HUMMING ALONG.

I must have died and gone someplace where hot, single men with British-ish accents know songs by my favorite band on the planet.

Someplace also known as heaven.

"Wait, wait, wait."

He stills, arm extended midair with a dangling ornament. "What?"

I point to my phone. "You know 'N Sync?"

"Oh, that. Force of habit. Chloe was obsessed when we were teens and made me learn all the songs and choreography. It's a bit humiliating, really."

It gets better and better. "Or your best feature."

"Come again now?"

I clasp my hands together in front of me as the music builds—inside and out. "Topher, I believe that 'N Sync is the single greatest band to have ever graced our little corner of the universe." I say all of this with utter seriousness because I DON'T JOKE ABOUT 'N SYNC. "And the fact that you know all the lyrics and dance moves just might make you the most perfect male specimen on the planet."

Then another thought occurs. "Wait. Were you at the concert?"

"Concert?" His voice hitches and I have him dead to rights.

"You were!" I clap my hands with the same glee as a child about to meet Santa Claus. "That's why you were near the arena the night we met, wasn't it?"

He gives a little shrug. "My sister would have murdered me if she knew I could have gone and experienced it in her stead. I did it for her. There was absolutely no pleasure in it for me."

I'm not buying it. But it doesn't matter. At best, he's a fellow 'N Sync fan. At worst, the best brother on the planet. If my gaze isn't showing off my acute desire for this man, I'd be surprised. (Can someone have bedroom eyes in the living room? I'm afraid that might be what's going on right about now.)

And then my hands go and betray me too—because I start fanning myself. I can't help it, though. This is an extreme turn-on and I just. cannot. even.

Topher looks me up and down, and his lips curl into a full-on smile.

Kill me now, folks. Mic drop. Lauren out. Next destination, the cemetery, 'cause it's no riddle—I'm dead, dead, dead.

And when he takes a step forward, curls his arm around my waist, and leans down, it's official. My heart just plain stops.

Especially when he opens his mouth and starts crooning.

It's not that the man has the best voice ever. He doesn't. But the lyrics and the spark in his eyes that I didn't expect ... whew.

Then he releases me and races to the kitchen, returning seconds later with two soup ladles. He tosses me one.

I laugh. This is so not where I saw my day going.

But the two of us spend the next five, ten—honestly, I don't know how long—minutes singing and dancing to the best 'N Sync songs. And there's just something about seeing a sexy man doing dance moves you salivated over in your teen years that is almost too hot to handle. He's got alllll the right moves. Not that he knows it. He's confident, but not arrogant, as he moves and spins and tosses back his head.

When we finally lower our ladles, our breath heavy from the spinning and jumping, we each wear a huge grin.

I prop my hand on my waist. "Now that didn't exactly scream dignity, did it?"

"Not at all." Shaking his head, he points his ladle at me. "But it was worth it to see you smile like that."

That's it, folks. You heard it right here first. Topher James is either going to be the best thing that ever happened to me—or my utter undoing.

eight

. . .

"I DEMAND to know where you're taking me, Tiger."

"Nope, nope, nope," I singsong back at him, pulling onto the freeway. It's the next day and I'm still flying high after our Christmas tree decorating slash impromptu 'N Sync karaoke last night, after which we sat on his couch and watched a few classic Christmas movies before I dragged myself home. (And before you get too excited, just know that Frederick decided to plop himself between us on the couch, so unfortunately, the evening did not turn romantic. But it was fun none-theless.)

Topher pokes and prods me but I refuse to break. I'm Alcatraz, baby. (Except for that time those three famous inmates escaped … but whatever.)

Finally, I pull into a crowded parking lot. "We're here."

Topher slips a ball cap on his head and shoves his sunglasses farther up his nose. It's not all that bright out, but maybe he has sensitive eyes. "And where is *here*, exactly?"

"Liberty Station. This morning, I read about an outdoor holiday market with a bunch of vendors selling everything from food to crafty stuff to toys to home goods. And it's this weekend only, so today is our last chance to go."

He scratches behind his ear and keeps looking at me, as if waiting for more. He's so darn cute when he isn't the one in control—it clearly flusters him.

I chuckle and pull my keys from the ignition. "I thought we could do that Christmas shopping you were talking about. You know, for the families at Shelby's school?" Rummaging in my purse, I pull out a list. "When I mentioned the idea this morning after breakfast, she gave me some details about what to look for."

At his continued quiet, I shift in my seat. Maybe he wasn't serious about all of this. It will probably be really costly, after all. "But we don't have to. I just thought …"

I start to tuck the list back into my purse, but his hand darts out to stop me. For a moment, I'm breathless as his fingers linger on the top of mine. Then he gently extricates the paper from my grip, looks it over.

And smiles. "I didn't think you *did* lists."

"You must be rubbing off on me." Winking, I unfasten my seatbelt and climb from the car.

He joins me and we make our way toward a large, tree-lined grassy area filled with what seems like hundreds of white easy-ups. Inside each makeshift booth sit anywhere from one to three tables, many with vintage and homemade signs describing what's for sale.

Christmas music plays from somewhere, nearly drowned out by the laughter of children running through the rows of booths and vendors hocking their wares.

It's midday, so the market is in full swing as we start walking up and down the aisles. I stop at a clothing booth and run my fingers along the silk of a brightly colored blouse that Alexis would love. One glance at the price tag has me deciding against that though. I'm guessing she'd rather me pay rent than spend my income on a gift for her.

As my eyes move along the table, I snort at the sight of light-up reindeer antlers mounted on a headband. Snagging one, I whip it onto my head and turn to Topher, grinning. "What do you think?"

He is completely stoic as he takes a step toward me. "I'm not sure—"

"Don't be a Scrooge, now." I shake a finger at him.

"What I was going to say"—he reaches toward the table just behind me—"I'm not sure the outfit is complete without this." Then he produces a red Rudolph nose that blinks and flashes.

"Ha ha, yes!"

He places it gently on my nose and I strike a pose. I'm sure I look completely ridiculous, but he must not be too embarrassed to be seen with me, because he's still here. And then he leans forward and whispers in my ear, "Prettiest reindeer *I've* ever seen."

Eek. "Well, I have to buy it now," I tease. "But only if you get a matching pair."

"That's going a tad too far, I think."

I take off the getup and turn to the vendor, a man in his sixties who genuinely could be Santa with his bushy white beard and evidence of one too many Christmas cookies around the middle. The guy grins as he rings up two pairs of antlers and two bulb noses.

Topher pulls out his credit card before I can protest.

The Santa man processes the payment and hands me the plastic bag. "You two are quite the adorable couple, if I may say so myself."

You may, sir. You may.

I glance at Topher, who—unlike a similar conversation with Denise while parasailing—doesn't contradict the man's statement. But I turn and smile sweetly. "Thank you, but we're not together like that." Maybe it's wrong of me, but I kind of want to gauge Topher's reaction.

A tiny frown flickers on his face and I cheer internally. Maybe after some time spent together, he's not so opposed to the idea as he was before.

We walk on and find some fabulous toys for the children on Shelby's list—wooden dolls, balls, and a variety of arts and crafts supplies, just to name a few. Topher makes a trip to my car to drop off our purchases while I keep shopping.

Then I see a booth that stops me in my tracks. A woman with short hair and a nose ring is sitting behind a table adorned with several large, framed photos as well as a catalog of prints in various sizes. Like a beacon, it calls to me and I make my way over.

Flipping through the prints, I find so many that I would love to take home and study. So many to inspire my own work. The orange-and-red sunset pictures taken along the beach are my favorite.

I look up to find the woman on her phone. "These are beautiful. Are you the photographer?"

She lowers her phone and tucks it away in the pocket of her jacket. "Thanks. I am." She points to the photo that's caught my eye. "Took that one just a few weeks ago over at Sunset Cliffs."

"It's gorgeous at night, isn't it?"

"Absolutely. And if you keep flipping, you'll find a few more of people who were there as well. I've also got a portfolio online of several shots that have already sold this morning in case you don't find something that strikes you right now."

"Are you kidding?" I run my finger along the outer edge of the sunset photo. Her mastery of light and depth is clear. "There are too many that strike me! I'm so impressed with your work. I wish my own photos would turn out like this."

"Oh, you're a photographer too?"

I wave a hand in dismissal. "Amateur. I don't even have a real camera, just my phone."

"Phones have a lot of great options these days." The woman pulls out her card and hands it to me. "If you ever want some recs for a great digital camera, though, text or email me."

"Wow, thank you." I see the price listed on the print and my heart falls. I'll definitely have to save up before I can afford it. Which means there's probably no way I could ever afford an actual camera. "I haven't even taken lessons. It's just something I enjoy doing on the side right now."

"There are a lot of great classes online now too." The woman holds up her hands and looks around. "And we're lucky to live somewhere with a lot of fodder for great pictures."

"How long have you been doing this?" Topher asks.

I nearly jump out of my skin because WHEN DID HE GET HERE? Glancing over, I find him looking at me. And even though I can't see his eyes behind his sunglasses, I feel their connection with me.

The woman looks between us and then shrugs. "About five years."

Whoa. The same as me, though she's obviously committed to her craft in a way I probably never will. "Well, you clearly have lots of talent."

We look for a bit longer, thank the woman, and head toward the food vendors at the far end of the quad.

"I didn't know you were a photographer."

I stick my hands into my jacket. "I'm not really. I just love taking pictures."

"I'd venture to say that makes you a photographer then." He shoulder bumps me as we walk.

The aroma of fried sugar fills my senses. "I appreciate your confidence in me, though it's greatly misplaced, I assure you. My stuff looks nothing like hers." Though I admit … I'd like for it to.

He waits a beat while we saunter. "What do you love about it?"

"I'm not sure, exactly. It's something I've always been drawn to. But over the last five years, it's become an urge that's really blossomed inside of me." I find that it's kind of cathartic to say this to him, since I really haven't told any of my friends. They know I snap away on my phone, but they likely assume that I just want to capture memories. And I do, but it's … more. "In many ways, it's saved my sanity. Given me something tangible to hold onto when I feel lost."

"What do you mean?"

"I don't know." I shake my head, my brow furrowed. "When something strikes me as beautiful or unique, I just have to capture it with my camera. To immortalize the world as I see it. I want to show the good and the bad—the truth, even when it's ugly. Does that make any sense?'

"It does, and it's admirable." Arriving at a Mexican food vendor selling the best-smelling empanadas ever, we join the short line. "A lot of photographers only seem to capture what they want to capture—to see what they want to see. To benefit off of lies or someone else's misfortunes."

There's bitterness in his voice. His confession makes me curious, but I don't want to push. And besides, I understand completely. "It's so easy for photographers —for people in general, really—to put out some version of the world that they've created instead of showing the world as it is."

That's what my mom does, anyway. Danny too.

"Yes, exactly." After a few beats of silence, he turns and grasps my elbow. "But that's not what you do, is it?"

I swallow at the contact. "I don't even put my photos

out there, so there's no chance they'll be misconstrued by anyone. I mean, I have one social account, but it's private. Just for me, you know?"

Before he can respond, it's our turn to order. I'm perusing the menu when I see movement out of the corner of my eye. It shouldn't distract me, because there's movement everywhere, but something catches my attention anyway.

Turning, I look—and do a double take. "Is that Freddy over there?" The man in question ducks behind a tree.

"Where?" Topher looks around me. He takes off his sunglasses and squints. "I don't see him."

"He went that way." I point.

"You going to order?" The poor guy inside the food truck wipes his sweating brow with the back of his forearm and scowls.

"Sorry," I say. We step out of line without ordering. "Topher? Was that Frederick I saw?"

"He didn't know we were coming here." His voice is tinged with ... something. I can't quite put my finger on it, but a strange prickle of unease wends through me.

No, my eyes must have been playing tricks on me. Even if he is super protective, Frederick would have no reason to follow us. It's not like *I'm* a threat of any sort to Topher.

"Okay, my mistake." I place a hand on my now-gurgling stomach. "I think it's time to feed me again. I'm like a little kid needing to eat every hour."

"All right." He flicks a smile my way. "But can we

select a different vendor? I'm afraid that one might spit in our food after we annoyed him like we did."

"You might be right." I follow the line of food vendors until I land on one from my favorite local falafel place. It always reminds me of New York when I eat there. Grabbing Topher's hand, I tug. "Come on. I know the perfect place."

Because Topher may be leaving soon, but in this moment, I want nothing more than to share my favorites, my memories with him. I use the digital camera in my mind to snap away as we navigate the crowd together, hand in hand.

Click.

As we eat falafel and laugh and breathe in the gorgeous winter air.

Click.

As we finish our shopping, high-fiving over completing our list—and our hands linger together a touch longer than necessary.

Click.

And as we pile back in the car and head to his place, where I tease him about having plans for tonight. As he leans against the door frame and asks with whom, and there's a bit of a jealous tinge to his voice.

And as I tell him it's with him—and Frederick and Shelby—and he steps forward, wraps me in a hug, and whispers that he looks forward to seeing me tonight.

Clickety click click click.

I'm a parade girl. Always have been, always will be. When we moved to NYC and attended the Macy's Thanksgiving Day Parade, I realized I wasn't the only one who loved the noise, the people, the magic that comes alive when thousands gather and present something beautiful and creative to the world.

So sitting here on a blanket near the Maritime Museum along the Embarcadero next to Topher, Frederick, and Shelby waiting for the Parade of Lights to pass us by, it's hard to believe that I have never attended before now.

It's almost like I've rediscovered a piece of me—a piece I left behind with my family.

I huddle into my jacket and pull my beanie farther down on my head. Tonight the breeze off the bay is more intense than usual—but still nothing compared with the early morning chill in Manhattan when waiting for hours in order to get a decent spot along that particular parade route.

Plus, I have a handsome man beside me giving off plenty of heat in his own jacket, scarf, and beanie. This time, I did remember gloves, although maybe I should have forgotten them on purpose …

Shelby breathes in the salty air. "It's so beautiful this time of night."

"It really is," I reply. The sun has drifted down from

the spot where it was when we first arrived two hours ago—according to Topher's research, the annual event attracts around one hundred thousand people and this is the best place to view the parade, which also meant we needed to get here early to claim our spot.

After our time at the market this morning, I chatted with my boss about my schedule since I can return to work in five days. Topher has been faithful to pay me for our "sessions," though I kind of feel guilty because I don't know that I've really done much to help him become a better manager.

Although right now, he's leaning back on his hands, head tilted up, his posture open and relaxed—so I guess maybe our time together has helped him loosen up, which was part of the goal too.

"When will the parade begin?" Frederick pulls a carrot from a plastic baggie and crunches on it.

"It already began at Shelter Island a while ago, so it should be making an appearance sometime soon," Topher replies.

"Was all that in the book your sister gave you?" I nudge him with my elbow, smiling.

"Some of it. I did a little extra research when you finally told me our destination."

When I dropped him at his house earlier this after-noon, it took me several minutes to reveal our exact plans for tonight. Teasing him is just so fun. "I have to keep you on your toes."

"You definitely do that, Tiger."

I can't help the blush that creeps over my cheeks, though it does nothing to warm my face, which at this point seriously feels like someone could carve an ice sculpture out of it. Slipping my jacket's hood over my beanie, I cross my arms in an attempt to get warmer.

Topher turns to me, his smirk in full array, and then tugs on the strings of my jacket so my hood tightens to a ridiculous degree. "Cold, love?"

"Just trying to be super stylish."

With a laugh, he slips his arm around my shoulder like it's NBD. (And for those who don't understand acronyms, that stands for No Big Deal. But it isn't no big deal. IT'S THE BIGGEST DEAL EVER.)

Then he tilts his chin down and lowers his voice. "Is this okay?"

"Mm-hmm." It's all I can say, because even though we've been friendly, maybe even a bit flirty now and again, I still can't suss out how he feels about me. Whether he sees this as … more. Or maybe this is how he treats all of his female friends. Since none of them live here, I won't have the opportunity to find out.

Thankfully, I am saved from thinking too hard about all of this, because a murmur rustles through the crowd. We see the lights in the distance first, just pinpricks really. Then the people around us seem to hush as the lighted boats approach, the excitement building and gathering like dewy beads of water on a leaf in the morning.

One after another, more than eighty sailboats, schooners, kayaks, and pontoons drift by just under the horizon. Some feature red and green lights, while others go classically white. Just like house yards, they're decked out in a variety of themes, from reindeers and snowmen to Christmas at the beach with inflatable palm trees and tiki lights. Together, the four of us exclaim over different favorites, laughing and ribbing each other for our choices.

And all the while, I snuggle against Topher, enjoying the strength of his embrace. At one point, my hand finds his knee. He hasn't said anything or asked me to move it, so you'd better believe I'm keeping it there for as long as I can.

When the last boat drifts away, I sigh. "That was amazing." And maybe I don't just mean the light parade.

"It really was," he says.

"Better than reading about it in a book, wasn't it?" I squeeze his knee before glancing up at him.

He waits a beat before answering. "Much."

"Well," Shelby says.

Both Topher and I startle at the intrusion of my friend's voice. I sit up a bit straighter and Topher drops his arm. It's suddenly very, very cold.

Standing, Shelby stretches. "That was so wonderful, but I have an early morning with thirty kiddos who will definitely have more energy than I do." Just to demonstrate her point, she yawns and quickly covers her mouth. "Lauren, are you ready to go? You're working early at the coffee shop tomorrow, right?"

"Well … yes. I am." But despite my four a.m. shift at Java Awakening, I have no desire to go home just yet.

"We can give you a ride back if you want to stay a bit longer," Topher says.

Nice to know he doesn't object to more time with

me, even though we've basically spent nearly every day together this week. "That sounds nice."

Shelby smiles knowingly. "I'll just be off then."

Frederick's gaze flickers between her and Topher.

Topher nods. "You should walk her to her car, mate. She's a woman alone and it's dark."

"I don't—"

"Oh, I'm fine," Shelby says, playing with the keys in her hand and staring at the ground.

But Freddy finally hops up. "No, no, I'd love to."

Topher and I also stand and fold up the blanket, which Shelby takes in her arms.

Nibbling her bottom lip, Shelby nods. "All right."

"I'll find you both afterward." Freddy gives Topher a friendly shove. "Have a care and keep your phone on this time, all right, mate?"

"Yeah, yeah."

With a wave, Shelby and Frederick walk off. There are lots of others exiting the area too, which leaves the place much quieter than it was just ten minutes ago.

I glance at Topher. "Up for a walk along the Embarcadero?"

"Why not?"

We stroll side by side for a bit along the harbor, passing boats hooked up to docks and bobbing in the bay. The cries of seagulls normally rampant during the day are strangely missing, leaving only the sound of passing cars and the lapping of water to accompany us. The moon is dim tonight and the stars take full stage against a black velvety blanket above.

Topher stops and looks out over the water. "I really

did have a lovely time tonight, Lauren. This morning as well."

"Me too." I set my hands on the railing in front of us. "It's nice to see you more relaxed."

"I am. And that's all thanks to you."

Something catches in his voice and it makes me turn to look at him. The stars are reflected in his eyes and I can't help but take another step closer.

He coughs and his right thumb presses into his left palm. "And your fantastic abilities as a tour guide, I mean."

Does he? Or is he afraid to push, to see if there could be more between us? To be honest, I'm tired of waiting, of wondering. It's exhausting, especially for someone who normally lets life guide her wherever it will.

Maybe he just feels limited by the professional nature of our relationship. Personally, I'd rather be poor than always wonder if he felt the same way about me as I do about him. So, I make a decision. "About that. I'm happy to keep being your tour guide to the area and help you relate better to your employees, but you're not allowed to pay me anymore."

He starts to protest and I lift my fingers to cover his lips. Oh goodness, and now I'm jealous of my own hand.

"It's not right, Topher. You're not just some stranger I knocked down in the street anymore. You're my ... friend."

His eyes seem to vibrate in the starlight as he takes me in. Almost everything inside is screaming at me to just grab the man and kiss him senseless like Kayla suggested, but another voice tells me to wait.

Miraculously, I listen to the second one.

Because I'm sure about him, but I want him to be sure too. And maybe that requires patience, but so be it. I will be the Mother Teresa of Patience if that's what it takes to have a man like Topher James.

I let my hand drop, but he quickly takes it and returns it to his mouth. His lips are warm and tender as he presses a kiss just below my knuckles. "*Just a friend?*"

I get the sudden urge to feel my own forehead, make sure I'm not feverish and hallucinating. Is this really happening right now?

I can't speak.

"Lauren, I've never met anyone quite like you." Topher holds the palm of my hand against the hard planes of his chest. His heart beats fast beneath my fingertips. "How in the world has no man scooped you up by now?"

Finally, the words come, a bit strangled but there. "Maybe I just haven't met the right one." I bite my lip. "Not that I've had much experience with dating lately."

"Surely the men of San Diego are complete morons if they've been ignoring *you.*"

His words are like tiny seductions, coaxing me to give more of myself, emotionally speaking. "I've gone on dates, but kept things light. Nothing serious."

"And why is that?"

"Well, my last boyfriend was a musician who dumped me when I was in the hospital so he could go back on tour. So there's that." I lift my eyebrows at him. "Now I'm turning the question around. Why has no woman scooped *you* up?"

His frown brings out tiny lines around his lips and I get the strong urge to kiss each one away.

"I was engaged a few years ago."

"What happened?" I gently prod.

"Elizabeth wanted to change me. She begged me to quit my job and be someone I wasn't. She didn't understand the years of tradition and what those meant to me, how deeply embedded they are in my core." He tucks a piece of hair behind my ear and I shiver. "I need someone who sees who I am and challenges me to be a better version of myself."

My tongue is thick as my blood whooshes in my ears. Honing that nun-like patience that doesn't come naturally at all, I wait for him to say that I am that woman.

But he doesn't. "Lauren, I wish I could be more like you. Your energy, your spunk, the way you seize the day—I admire them more than you know. Conversely, I tend to overthink everything."

"Not *you*." I smile so he knows I'm teasing.

He's not playing, though. "How do you do it? Allow yourself to let go and just … feel?"

"It's how I'm wired, I guess." My hand closes, fisting his jacket. "Please just tell me. What are you feeling right now, Topher? Because I know how *I* feel … about you."

And there it is, the truth hanging between us. Guess I'm not winning any peace prizes for patience anytime soon, but at least I've said my piece. The ball is his to move now.

After what feels like a thousand rotations around the sun, he gives his head a tiny shake. "It doesn't matter what I feel. I can't in good conscience pursue anything with you beyond friendship."

My grip loosens. "Why not?"

Topher sets his forehead against mine and we stand like that for hours, days, months, or so it seems, before he speaks. "Lauren, if I were any other man … but I'm not. I'm me. And you're you." He pulls away, straightens, and drops my hand.

My whole body is as heavy as sludge. "I don't understand."

He runs a hand through his hair and huffs out a sigh tinged with frustration. "I know, and that's my fault." Then he stuffs his hands into his pockets. "We just … wouldn't be a good fit. We want different things."

No, we don't. I want him. And it seems like maybe he wants me. Can't we figure the rest out?

"Come on. It's time to get you home."

So his mind is made up, then.

Blinking and without a word, I follow him down the well-lit path, my heart trying to make sense of the waning it feels.

nine

IT'S BEEN five days since Topher and Frederick dropped me off at my front door after the parade, and I haven't heard a word from them since. Not that I care about hearing from Frederick—he's a nice enough guy.

But Topher ... I thought we had at least the spark of something starting.

"Lauren, I've never met anyone quite like you."

"If I were any other man ..."

Why would he say those things unless he felt something for me?

"We just ... wouldn't be a good fit. We want different things."

That seems like a paltry excuse. Maybe he doesn't think his family would approve of me. They're dignified and I'm definitely not. They run an impressive corporation and I ... well, I'm standing here alongside Kayla making my hundredth americano for the day, a stained apron around my neck and a pair of worn Chuck Taylors on my feet.

It's almost the end of my six-hour shift, and I've grown immune to the pep that the scent of ground coffee beans usually infuses into me. The whirr of the grinder at least has the decency to drown out my thoughts—and the impatient huffing of a twenty-something Little Miss Thang in her leopard-print fur jacket and tight jeans who's looking at her pink-bedazzled phone and smacking on some gum.

"Is my coffee ready yet?" she whines.

The trusty old grinder has failed me. That, or she has an extraordinarily high-pitched voice. I turn and force a smile. "Almost!"

"Unbelievable. I've been waiting for, like, twenty minutes."

"It's been five," I snap. "Five minutes." And that is actually on the longer side of what any customer has to wait around here, and only because the line has been out the door all day long. I'm not sure what it is about the Friday before all the schools go on Christmas break, but the whole city has seemed extra crowded and busy wherever I go.

"Hey. You can't be rude to me like that. I'm the customer."

I really, really want to take this coffee and show her what I think about her customer-ness, but instead I grit my teeth and slide the coffee across the bar. "Here."

"You can bet with this level of service, I won't be back," the woman practically screeches. Then she turns on a heel and leaves.

"Argh," I growl as I turn to Kayla, who has just finished serving an elderly couple—blessedly the last ones in what has been a never-ending line. "Why are some people such jerks?"

"Right? It's been a day."

"How's it going out here?" And that would be Josh, Kayla's husband and the Java Awakening manager, coming through the swinging door that leads to the kitchen. He's wearing his usual—a *Star Wars* Who's Your Daddy? T-shirt, a long-sleeved flannel over top, and thick-rimmed glasses. A beanie covers his brown hair.

"Nothing we can't handle, Solo." Kayla winks at him.

"I don't doubt it for a moment, Leia." Chuckling, Josh approaches, his eyes never leaving his wife's. He's looking at her like she's a freaking goddess and he's her most faithful worshiper. And when he curls his hand around her waist and pulls her in for a kiss, it's like they're at their very own private temple.

That's what I want. A man who knows his own mind and goes after what he wants. Who thinks I'm worth figuring things out with. And I won't settle for anything less than that.

Topher obviously wasn't that man. So what? That's all right. Someday, the One will call to me. I just hope I'm not too old and deaf to hear him when he finally does.

I'd laugh at the picture forming in my mind if the urge to cry wasn't stronger.

This is so stupid. It's only been two weeks since I

saved Topher from that car. And even though my chest feels tight and my eyes have cried all the tears and I've eaten chocolate like it's Halloween night and I'm a teenager with an extremely high metabolism, you can't fall in love in two weeks.

So I'll just keep pressing forward. I'll get past this.

I will.

Since there's still no line at the counter, I turn away from the newlyweds and start cleaning the espresso machine. Finally, they come up for air and remember where they are.

"Welcome back," I say dryly.

Kayla throws her head back and laughs. "Sorry."

"Don't be." I soften my voice. "I'm glad you're happy."

"And we're glad you're here." My friend approaches and slips her arm into mine.

"Me too." I turn to Josh. "Thanks again for giving me the extra hours this week. The timing couldn't have been better."

"I'm glad they opened up, although I'm going to have to talk with my wife here about scaring off our temp workers."

Kayla makes a face at him. "If you hired some competent people, I wouldn't have to scare them off."

He lowers his glasses and looks at her over the rim. "Maybe we need to discuss this further in my office."

"Maybe we do," she replies in an incredibly suggestive tone.

"Gross, you guys." I hip bump Kayla away from me. "I'm right here."

We all laugh and Josh does head back to do paperwork in his office, leaving Kayla and me to prepare for the upcoming lunchtime rush. I'm dragging a bit, but Hannah, my replacement, should be arriving soon anyway. Then I can go back to my bed and watch some cycling videos to prepare for my first class back at the gym tomorrow.

And, yeah, maybe finish off the bag of Hershey kisses hidden under my comforter. (I know there's an irony in watching workout videos while consuming candy, but I can't handle your judgment right now, mmm-kay?)

As we clean dishes and ready our supplies, Kayla chats about the upcoming wedding in four days. "Evie is starting to freak out about the details a little bit, but I've tried to remind her all that matters at the end of the day is being married to the guy she loves."

"So you aren't sad you didn't get a full-blown wedding?" Kayla would have made such a gorgeous bride—so elegant too.

"Sometimes, but then I think about all the family stuff. Like, would my dad walk me down the aisle? I feel like it would have been too soon for that, you know? We just reconciled. And as things stand with my mom, I'm not sure I would want the two of them in the same room together."

"I totally get that."

"So …" She trails off.

I quirk an eyebrow. "So, what?"

"Have you heard from him yet?"

"Him who?" I plunge my hands into soapy bubbles

a bit too aggressively. A surge of bubbles rushes over the side and soaks my apron. I ignore the spill and start scrubbing away on the outside of a plastic blender. "I just don't get it, Kay. He was starting to open up. We were getting along, laughing, smiling, sharing things about our lives, our families. And then, he just … shut it all down."

"Remind me again what exactly he said."

As I finish up the dishes, I recount my conversation with him on Sunday night. Then I dry my hands on a towel.

"Sounds to me as if he likes you, but he's scared for some reason." Her face is a mask of concentration. "Or it really could be that he's leaving and doesn't see how it could ever work. You'd never move, would you?"

"*I don't think I'd ever leave San Diego, to be honest.*" I cringe as I recall my words while decorating his Christmas tree. Though maybe lately I've been rethinking them.

"I wouldn't want to, but for love? Not that we're in love or anything. As of last weekend when we were actually talking, I'd only known him like nine days." After checking to make sure we still don't have any new customers, I tug on the ends of my hair and lean back against the counter.

"I've coached couples who fell in love much more quickly than that." Kayla holds up her soapy hands. "Not saying it happens a lot, but I do think it's possible to feel something deep and real after not that long. It doesn't *always* take people years to figure out that they're supposed to be together." She smiles, and I know she's thinking about her and Josh.

"You might be right, but there's one problem."

"What's that?"

"Topher made it pretty clear that things can't go any further between us. And I'm not going to be one of those girls who obnoxiously chases a man."

"Girls can grand gesture too."

"But that's not what this would be. This would be me not respecting his wishes. If he wants me, he's going to have to come and find me."

A bell rings at the door. I turn—and freeze at the sight of Topher in the doorway as if I've summoned him. He's wearing that sweatshirt with the hood up again, plus sunglasses even though he's now inside and looks a little silly.

But he's here. And the fact his sweeping gaze settles in my direction means that maybe he's here … to see me?

"Someone's ears were burning." Kayla pokes me in the side. "Go on, talk to him. Your shift is basically over anyway. I'll cover till Hannah gets here."

"Are you sure?"

"Absolutely."

With a quick hug goodbye, I unhook my apron and hand it to her, then round the counter. Topher and I meet in the middle of the lobby.

"Hi, Lauren."

"Topher." I shift from one foot to the other. "I see you found my second job location."

"I thought this was your third job."

My nose scrunches. I guess technically he's right, which only annoys me. Tilting my head, I peer up at him. "What are you doing here?"

Glancing around as if making sure no one is looking at us—a ridiculous notion, since most of the people here have in earbuds or are speaking with someone else at their individual tables—he lowers his sunglasses. "I missed you."

My stomach flops. "You did?"

"Yes, and ..." He removes the hood and rubs the back of his neck. His hair is sticking out on the side and it's adorable and I wonder if he's had that cowlick since he was a young boy—and oh! What if his kids end up having it too? That would be so adorable, especially if they're *my* kids too.

Whoa, whoa, whoa. Rein it in, girl.

I inhale deeply. "And ...?"

He reaches for my hand and intertwines my fingers with his. "And I was wondering if I could take you somewhere."

"Somewhere?" Ugh, why can't I say coherent things? But my brain is pinging nonsensical data at me. Because despite saying his feelings about me were irrelevant, here he is, asking me to go ... where? On a date?

"I want to show you something. And talk."

Talk.

Okay. I can work with that.

I nod and his whole face blossoms before my eyes.

He breathes out what can only be a sigh of relief, then leans in and quickly kisses me on the cheek. "Are you ready to leave now, love?"

I thought you'd never ask.

That's what I want to say. What I do say? "You got it."

Then my stupid clicky finger gun comes back out and I'm dying as I hear Kayla cackle at me from behind the counter. As Topher leads me out, I turn quickly to Kayla, stick out my tongue, then mouth "Oh my gosh" in an exaggerated fashion to her.

She responds with a kissy face and I roll my eyes, walking out of Java Awakening with the first hopeful steps I've taken all week long.

Torrey Pines State Natural Reserve is a glorious wilderness filled with sandstone cliffs, plant life, and majestic views of the beach and ocean below.

I'm not sure how I've managed to live in San Diego for five years without exploring it before, but I know this won't be the last time. On the ride over, Topher was fairly quiet, only speaking when I asked him about his week. It sounded pretty tame after all the activities we shoved into the week before, because all he did was read next to the fireplace and our Christmas tree.

That's what he said—*"our Christmas tree."*

I nearly swooned into a puddle right there in his car.

But I held it together enough to detail my week for him—mostly working and getting ready for Evie's wedding. I held back some of the more intimate details like shopping for her lingerie, but I told him about the final dress fittings and the late nights of pizza and boxed wine while watching a slew of romcoms with my besties and making centerpieces for the reception.

I also refrained from giving him the deets on my pathetic attempts at not missing him.

By the time we reached Torrey Pines, things were a bit more comfortable between us, though I still have no clue what he wants to "talk" about. Then we drove up the side of a mountain and parked near a trailhead, and I turned to him and asked if this hike was in his book. He winked at me, hopped out of the car, and—like the nearly-British gentleman he is—opened my door.

After about one minute on the trail, I had my phone out. Now, as we hike, I take pictures of the trees, stark against the horizon—some holding onto the sides of the cliff for dear life. But they've dug in and they're strong and I can't help but admire their tenacity.

I photograph the sand and the rocks at our feet, spying a scampering beetle and clicking away.

I capture the rays of light breaking through the clouds, landing on the water in this incandescent way that has my insides burning and wishing I could scoop them up in my fingers, carry them home with me.

And when we come to a pile of dead trees, with a sign that says they've been ravaged by drought and other forms of nature, I squat and take pictures of that too.

The good. The bad. The ugly. It's all part of this place's story and worthy of being told.

After about a half-hour of hiking on the deserted

trail, we approach an outlook, all alone except for the cliffs to the left, the ocean spread out like butter in front, and a clump of sprawling Torrey pine trees behind us. Finally, to my right is Topher—which means that it's three hundred and sixty degrees of gorgeous scenery around me.

I aim my camera at him and click. He flinches a bit, so I flip to selfie mode and hold the phone out in front of us. "Smile."

Before I can snap the photo, he steps forward and wraps his hands around my waist from behind, leaning down so his head is right next to mine. And there's Mr. Dimple in all his glory, along with Topher's gentle smile.

I snap, capturing the moment before I can wake from this dream. Lowering the camera, I stay in his arms. "Thank you for bringing me here, Topher."

"I was hoping you'd be able to find some inspiration for your photos."

"It would be hard not to."

"The height doesn't bother you?"

Aw, he remembered my fear on the parasailing boat. "No. There's enough cushion between the trail and the drop. And right now, I'm fine."

Probably because he's holding me. I'm secure. Safe.

And no way am I moving a muscle.

We stay like that for a while, the wind blowing strands of my hair back against him. He brushes it to one side, his finger sliding along the base of my neck in the process. "Lauren …"

"Yeah?"

"Would you let me see your photos?" A pause. "It's all right if you'd rather n—"

"Here." There's no hesitation for me. Maybe there should be, but there's just … not. Even if I don't know everything about this man, I trust him. And after Danny, that's kind of a miracle. Holding up my phone in front of us, I take a breath and open it to my social media page. Then I begin to scroll.

"Slow down." One of his hands cups mine and he brings the phone closer. His large thumb scrolls through the photos. Meanwhile, his other hand is still firmly secured around my waist. And whether he realizes it or not, his fingers curl and uncurl against my stomach like a gentle massage.

Several moments later, when he's yet to speak a single word, I nibble my lip. "Well?"

"Well, I'm no photographer myself, but I'd say you're very talented, love."

Does he realize what it does to my whole being when he calls me that? Probably not. "You think so?"

I feel his nod against my cheek. "I love seeing the world through your eyes. It's so much more exciting than my own."

"I think your eyes are very exciting."

His deep chuckle resonates against me. "I'm serious, though. You shouldn't hide a talent like that. You should share it with the world."

"I can't."

"Lauren, you value authenticity, and yet you're hiding some of the best parts of yourself away from the world. Why?"

I stiffen for a moment, then relax. He's right—I do value authenticity. So how can I explain my stance on this? "I just don't want the thing I love to become the thing that eventually destroys my life."

"Ah. Like your mum?"

I nod.

"You aren't her, love."

"I know. So why tempt fate by going after a dream? By showing the world my talent, as you call it?" What happens if I become so obsessed with it that my priorities shift—for the worse?

"Because talent like yours, when given freely and with the right motives, makes the world a better place. You can inspire people. You've certainly inspired me."

Oh, Topher. I snuggle back against him. "Thank you. That means a lot."

"So you'll consider it?"

Lowering the phone, I peek back at him. "You're awfully pushy for someone who won't even tell me what he does for a living." It's meant as a tease, but I can tell by the way his arms tighten around me that he took it as a barb.

A challenge.

Well, maybe that *is* how I meant it. Why is it fair for me to tell him everything about my life while he shares only bits and pieces?

But before I can say more, he begins to speak. "My job. That's … complicated. Suffice it to say that I wish I was as talented in my profession as you are at everything you seem to do."

"What are you talking about? Topher, you're so

smart. And I don't know of anyone as dedicated as you are."

I twist in his arms so I'm facing him—and just like that, we're back in the same place we were on Sunday night. But this time, I'm hoping for a very different outcome.

Tucking my phone into the back pocket of my jeans, I loop my hands around his neck. "You're constantly trying to be better at your job. I don't know very many people who are so passionate about serving their employees."

His green eyes are a torrent, a hurricane, and there's a storm brewing below the surface. "I work so hard because I need to. Even though I desire to be, I'm not the right man for the job—at least, my father doesn't think so."

"What makes you think that?"

He swallows. "When I was a lad, maybe thirteen, I overheard him saying he worried I'd never be ready, that the job was just so demanding, and he feared I wasn't going to be able to handle it."

What kind of person worries so much about their young son taking over a business before he's even shaving? "Maybe he just meant that it's a difficult job and would be hard for anyone. It's not necessarily a reflection on you."

"I wish that was it. But he specifically said he worried my temperament wouldn't be able to handle it."

"You said the two of you are a lot alike. So maybe he sees what a toll it takes on him and he doesn't want the same for you." I tilt my head. "Still, if it troubles you so much, would it be such a bad thing to find your own path—something of your own choosing, that makes you come alive?"

"Even if that *was* possible, I would still choose this. I want to serve my people—that is, my employees —well."

"And you've dedicated your life to reading books about it. But Topher, books can only get you so far."

"So you keep reminding me."

"And I mean it. Relationships are built by opening yourself up, by spending time with people, by figuring out what makes them tick—by observation, yes, but also just by asking them." I play with the zipper on his jacket. "And that might require you to step out of your comfort zone, out from behind your books. But if the last two weeks have shown you anything, isn't it that you're fully capable of that? Because I see a man in front of me who is the full package—humble, but eager to serve—which is exactly what a leader should be."

My monologue over, I press my lips together so he has time to respond.

He just stares at me for a long while, and I wonder if he's actually heard anything I've said. But then, he speaks. "Tiger, you are without a doubt the most encouraging, wonderful woman on the planet."

I bite my lip and smile. "You think so, huh?"

"I know so. And well, I'm rather mad about you. I shouldn't have left the other night. I was a blasted fool to walk away. But I've wanted to tell you something for a while now. Something that I'm sure will change how you feel about me—if you even feel the same way I do, which maybe you don't."

"Rest assured, Topher James, that I'm kind of mad about you too." I take his confession as permission to run my fingers through the hair at the nape of his neck, something I've been dying to do since we met. He shudders at my touch. "And nothing is going to change my mind about that."

"But that's just it. This something is rather large, actually, and it makes things all the more complicated. And it's always affected my relationships in the past."

"What? Are you a bad kisser or something?" My right index finger trails to his cheek and presses the spot where I know his dimple is hiding. "Because we can work on that."

He barks out a laugh. "Well, no one's ever told me I am, but I'm sure you could give me a few pointers nonetheless."

"Happy to any time." Seriously. What's the guy waiting for, an invitation written in gold lettering? *Kiss me, dude.*

But he just sighs and looks out at the ocean, which is tossing and turning. "It has nothing to do with my kissing ability." A distant bolt of lightning flashes in the clouds coming this way. I pray it's not a bad omen.

"Then what?"

"It's about who I am." Then he swings his gaze back toward me. "Who my family is."

Is that all? "Topher, we all have a past. I have secrets and crazy family drama too, but they don't define me. And yours don't have to define you." I place my hand over his heart. "Right now, we can just be Lauren and Topher. We don't have to put a label on anything or delve into the past. That doesn't matter."

"You have no idea how badly I want that to be true."

"So make it true. Let go and just … feel."

"You don't know what you're saying."

"Yes, I do."

He hesitates. "Are you … sure?"

"Abso-freaking-lutely."

With a laugh, he tucks me into his arms and leans down so his mouth is next to my ear.

And once again, I'm holding him around the neck.

"Lauren, you're like a rare jewel of light. I didn't know I was standing in the darkness till I met you." His breath is warm against my ear, his whispers sweeter than all the chocolate in the world piled sky-high. "I don't know if I can give you what you want or need, but all I know is … I just wanna be with you."

Did the man just speak to me in 'N Sync lyrics?

I think I'm in love.

That feeling continues as Topher's lips find my own —and they taste like honey, just the way I thought they would. His hands cup my face as he kisses me sweetly. Then he begins to pull away much too soon, but I'm not having any of that. I tug him back to me and increase the intensity of our kiss—and he all too willingly complies.

I feel like I could kiss this man forever, but when I hear the clearing of throats and some raucous laughter behind us, I know it's time to go. Breaking away, I turn my head and glare at a group of teenage boys who move along quickly at the sight of an angry Lauren Bear.

Topher steps back, nearly stumbling and grasping onto me to steady us both. Then he runs a hand down his face to shake away the awestruck look on his face. "Lauren, maybe we …"

But no way am I letting him say that shouldn't have happened. I pop up on my tiptoes and brush my lips against his again. "You were right," I whisper. "The problem is definitely *not* your kissing."

With a wink, I skip off down the trail, leaving him to chase me, laughter in our wake.

ten

I'M BACK at the gym and it feels so right.

Especially when Topher is here.

"Come on, ladies and gents. You've got this." I'm up front in my cycling shorts and tank, pumping away at my bike as we climb a fake hill. My legs burn deliciously and my heart is racing to the tune of "Here We Go." The seats in front of me are filled with my faithful Saturday morning students, many of whom mauled me with hugs, saying they missed me so much and that the replacement teacher wasn't nearly as fabulous as me.

And while I hate when others are put down, I'll admit that their loyalty did my heart good.

"Tackle this hill! Climb, climb, climb!" I use my silly singsong voice, which reverberates from the head mic I'm wearing through the speakers.

The room is rather warm today, making my tank stick to my chest. Ugh, boob sweat is the worst ever. This always seems to happen in the winter. People are freezing when they hustle inside and expect a warm space. But as soon as they begin working out, it gets unbearably hot, especially back in the group fitness rooms.

The heat and our current intensity level have everyone huffing and puffing—including Topher and Frederick, who are in the back row. I grin at the thought of giving two super buff guys a workout that's kicking their tight butts. I'm flying that he's here—and yeah, maybe it's got me working my people a little harder than usual, just to show off what I can do.

But the encouragement will never stop. "I know you guys are tired. Dragging. You don't think you have another quarter-mile in you, much less a whole mile. But you can do this. You are strong." *Pump pump.* "You are fierce." *Pump pump.* "And you. Are. Brave."

As we crest the top of a proverbial hill, I hear a collective sigh of relief and a few whoops.

"All right, gang. Time to cool down." I lead the group in a round of exercises to lower their heart rates and stretch their tired muscles, then give a clap. "Thanks for a great class today. You brought your A game. And even though I know it's just so you can go to Christmas parties this weekend and eat your weight in pie and chocolate, I'm proud of you."

Everyone laughs as I cut the music and pull my mic off my sweaty head. Whew. I get out my clipboard where I'm supposed to tally the number of students we had, and then take a quick looksie at my schedule. That was my last class out of three this morning. I've got several tomorrow and then a few days off for Evie's wedding festivities on Monday and Tuesday.

Before I can think any more about my schedule, I glance up to find Topher walking toward me like he's just ridden a horse for three days straight. He's got a slight limp and is walking bowlegged.

I set my clipboard down. "Did I ride you a little hard this morning?" Then I realize how *that* sounds and my eyes widen as I bite my bottom lip.

But he just laughs, his eyes full of mirth as he straightens out and walks normally toward me, wrapping me in a sweaty hug. How does the guy still smell so good after an hour in this sauna of a classroom? It's unnatural how his body spray and deodorant overpower any sort of sweaty stench.

Me on the other hand? Gag.

Oh, well. I push against his chest and angle for a quick kiss. "Thanks for coming." I peek around him and find Frederick leaning against the back wall, talking with some girl in a pink sports bra and little booty shorts. "Looks like Freddy is doing all right."

"We both had a great time. You're really good at this too—not that I'm surprised." Topher leans in for another kiss. "Are you available for lunch?"

"I need to grab a quick shower first, but yes, that sounds great."

Someone behind us clears her throat and we separate to find Instagirl there. The blonde twenty-something is a regular in my class. Her real name is Brittney and she's got some huge social media following—in fact, she's the reason why Kayla's dating coach business got off to a rocking start.

But right now, something squirms in my belly at the sight of her phone, which she's holding up. She's not taking a photo, is she? "Do you need something, Brittney?"

My voice comes out strangled with an edge of panic. I know it's unreasonable. Even if she were to post a picture of me, there's hardly a chance my past would find me. At least, I don't think so. Still. I don't want the media taking control of my story's narrative ever again.

Brittney lowers her phone and points at Topher. "You look really familiar. Have we met?"

Topher's grip on my waist tightens. "No." And he doesn't make any move to introduce himself either. The stiff, regal posture is back.

And just at that moment, Frederick swoops in. "Ready to go, mate?"

Brittney glances between them, tapping her phone against her lower lip. "Love the accents. Okay, maybe we haven't met, because I'd remember *that*." She flips her long hair over her shoulder. "Maybe I've seen you online. Are you a content provider like me?"

"Brittney, this is my ... friend, and he's visiting from K—"

"Time to go." Frederick has now fixed Topher with a glare and juts his chin toward the Exit. Why is he being so forceful? I thought they didn't have plans.

Topher nods, then turns and gives me a peck on the cheek. "Message me when you're ready for lunch and we'll meet somewhere, yeah?"

"Sure." My forehead scrunches as they start to leave. Then I turn to Brittney. "You didn't take any photos of me, right? I don't want my picture posted online." My voice echoes and Topher looks back at me, something piercing in his gaze.

She rolls her eyes. "I know your rule. I just got a few pics of *him*." Lifting her phone, she scrolls, then frowns. "They're blurry, though. But I'll remember where I know him from eventually."

Why would she know him? He doesn't even live here. "Maybe he just has one of those faces."

"Maybe." She purses her lips together like she doesn't believe me, then shrugs and flounces from the room.

I'm still scratching my head about the whole thing as I head home, shower, and text Topher. He asks if we can meet at his place, so I drive over. The midday sun is warm on my skin—a nice change from the cloudy days of late—as I climb from my car and walk up to his house.

I haven't been back here since we decorated the tree, and when he opens the door, I get a peek at our creation from the front door. Even though it's only two in the afternoon, he's got the thing lit up. There are even a few presents sitting underneath. I wonder who those are for, since he's not sticking around for Christmas.

Or maybe … maybe he's changed his mind? A tiny thrill races through me at the thought of spending Christmas with him.

As I give him a hug, I sense a tautness to his shoulders—his whole body, really. "You okay?" I look up at his face, and he's wearing a tight expression, a frown. And there's something deeply troubled in his eyes. "What's wrong?"

He releases me and blows out a breath as he walks into his living room. "I have to tell you something."

I chuckle. "This sounds serious."

"It is."

Oh. I set my purse on the table. Suddenly the cozy room feels too small, claustrophobic, and I don't want to have this conversation anywhere near our tree—not where so many happy memories were born. "Let's go outside then."

"Won't you be cold?"

"You can keep me warm." I try a wink, but he either doesn't see it—or doesn't want to react to my playfulness. I fold my arms over my chest and follow him through the kitchen and out the back door onto the beach. What could have changed between this morning —when he was so playful and carefree—and now?

Once again, the private beach is deserted, a land of sparkling sand unto itself. The water is a comforting constant as we walk a little way and sit on the sand.

Before he can speak, I ask the question burning in my mind. "Are you overthinking things again?" Because maybe he's once again realized that there would be logistical problems with him living in Kentonia and me living here. "I know we just started this thing between us, and we still don't have to put any labels on it, but I'm happy to visit you overseas. I've always wanted to see Europe. And you can show me around. I still don't know much about your country because I've been waiting for *you* to tell me more about it."

And it strikes me again, how little I know about him and his personal life. But I know that he likes green tea and that he enjoys being in nature when he takes the time. I know that he gets these little crinkle lines around his eyes when he allows himself to really and truly smile. I know he has this deep, beautiful soul that challenges me and makes me contemplate doing things I've never done before—things that I've run away from.

I know that he makes me feel brave.

And those things—not his family or his profession or where he's from—are what matter to me. It's those kinds of details that make up a person. Besides, given our whirlwind relationship, I can't possibly be an expert on all things Topher James.

Yet.

Those details, that knowledge, will come as we spend more time together.

Unless he's about to dump me, in which case …

Don't even go there, Lauren.

He brings his knees up and wraps his arms loosely around them, looking not at me but the horizon. "Kentonia is a wonderful place. I've lived there all my life. It's green in the summer and gorgeous in the fall and there are mountains capped with snow in the winter."

"That does sound wonderful." Unlike his view, I'm watching him, taking him in.

"And, like England, it has a … monarchy."

"Oh, like a queen?"

"And a king. And a princess." Then he looks at me, his face smooth and serious. "And a prince."

I blink at him, waiting for him to continue. When he doesn't, I let loose a chuckle. "Okay, what else?"

His right hand massages his left—something I've noticed him doing before when he's nervous. But why is he nervous to tell me more about his country? "The prince's name is Christopher Alexander James Huntington." He pauses. "And someday, when his father has died or stepped down from the throne, he will be king."

"That's usually how it works, right?" Something he's said is bothering me, though. It's niggling the back of my mind like a worm trying to break free of soil.

"Yes." He shakes his head. "About a month ago, the prince had a bit of a mental breakdown and was sent to California by his parents to rejuvenate."

The proverbial worm surges to the surface, spraying dirt everywhere.

My jaw drops. What is he saying?

"And he never intended to, but he met a beautiful woman who changed everything for him." Topher scoots closer to me, grabs my hand. "Lauren, I should have told you, but—"

I push his hand away and scramble to my feet. "Are you serious right now? You're a …" I can't even say the word. Is this a dream? Surely, this isn't real. Girls like me don't meet princes. And princes in real life are balding and pale and … not Topher.

He joins me in standing. "A prince. Yes."

"This isn't happening. I need … to go." My head

pounds and I start jogging down the beach. Because what in the freaking world is going on?

I hear his footsteps behind me and increase my speed. I run for a half-mile or so, but my feet will never be able to outrun my heart.

And as tempting as it is to run away just like I always do, I need answers.

I whirl around and he's there, not far behind me. We both bend over, our hands on our upper thighs as our breath comes deep and fast.

Then I fling the words I've been thinking at him. "So, you've just been messing with me this whole time? Laughing behind my back about the American girl falling all over herself because she met a prince and doesn't even know it?" Oh man, I've been such an idiot.

"No!" He rushes to me, pressing his cold fingertips against my cheeks as he looks into my eyes. "It was more refreshing than you know to be around someone who saw me—not my family, not what I was born into, but who I am. Someone who believes in me and helps me to be a better man. You don't let me off the hook for anything, and I adore you for it."

He makes me better too. But … "You lied to me."

"I should have told you before now—I know that. But I didn't want you to see me differently, treat me differently." His thumb trails the crescents under my eyes and I shiver. "I wanted to go on being just Topher and Lauren."

"But we're not. I may be Lauren, but you're not just Topher. You're Prince Christopher." Spitting the words out, I turn them over in my brain. They just don't compute. It doesn't sound or feel like *my* Topher. "Your life is public, isn't it? You probably have people analyzing your every move, taking your picture, shaping the narrative every single day."

I shake away from his touch because I can't focus with his skin scorching my own.

"I'll admit, that's part of the job. An unfortunate part." He looks so miserable as he kicks at the sand. The airborne grains scatter on the breeze. "I know that you said we didn't have to divulge more about ourselves than we were comfortable doing. But when I saw that woman today asking questions—and your reaction when you thought she'd taken your photo—I knew I had to tell you the whole truth. Please, love. Forgive me."

Forgive him? Maybe someday.

But right now? Where can we possibly go from here? I don't even know what he wants. "Was this all just some fling to you?" *Because I was half in love with you already.*

"Not at all." He steps toward me again, closing the gap. "Lauren, I have never felt for a woman the way I feel about you."

"How is that possible? I mean, you were engaged, Topher. Or was that a lie too?"

He winces and shakes his head. "Yes, I was engaged, and I thought it was love at the time. But it wasn't this give and take that we have. This mutual respect, this challenge and acceptance. Have you ever felt as connected to anyone as this? Because I know I haven't."

I don't want him to know I feel his argument to my

toes, that I want nothing more than to run to him and forget about the fact he's a prince. That he lied. That he's just as fake as my mother and Danny were.

But before I can say anything else, I catch sight of movement in the distance—someone else standing there. I point. "Why is Frederick following us?"

Topher glances back, then sighs. "He's my protection detail."

A bodyguard? I groan. Of course they wouldn't send a prince across the ocean without some sort of protection. Now all of his strange behavior makes sense. Another thought strikes. "He doesn't want us together, does he? All those times he insisted on tagging along, how he sat between us when watching movies."

"It's just his job to keep me safe, and he wanted to be sure you weren't a threat. He told me I should keep my distance, that things would come to nothing, and I tried. But the pull you have on me … I told you. I couldn't stay away."

"Well, maybe you should have."

"Tiger—"

"Stop!" My brain is pure sludge, but one fact shines through. Topher was right.

Our feelings really *are* irrelevant. We really *do* want different things. Because I've lived my life in the spotlight once, and I have no wish to do it again.

"I'm sorry." I step away, my hands up. "But I need time to process this."

"Take all the time you need, love."

Except I can't take all the time, can I? Because he

leaves in less than a week to go home to the country his family runs.

It's all too much.

I shake my head and start walking back to the house. He follows, keeping a respectful distance behind me, not saying a word.

eleven

. . .

I DON'T CARE that it's December nineteenth or that
it's sixty degrees outside.

Ice cream therapy knows no limits.

Somehow I managed to drag myself out of bed this
morning and dig deep to talk some verve into my
cycling students, but as soon as the last class ended, I
slumped it home and directly to the freezer. That's when
I settled right here on our living room couch, torturing
myself with romcom movies as I shove bite after bite of
Sour Patch ice cream into my mouth.

The irony? I don't even like Sour Patch ice cream.
And it's not even mine—it's Alexis's. Hopefully she will
take pity on me and offer forgiveness when she sees
what a sorry state I'm in.

Because the man I was falling for is not what he
seemed.

But it's not Alexis who finds me. It's Shelby. She
enters the room and halts at the sight of me curled in a

blanket, tears streaming down my face as I listen to Tom Cruise tell Renee Zellweger that she completes him.

"Lies!" I throw a pillow at the television.

"Aw, Laur," Shelby soothes as she grabs the remote from the arm of the couch and flicks off the movie. Then she sits down beside me and squeezes my arm. "It's going to be okay."

And I don't even care that she's totally using her kindergarten teacher voice, because right now, I need to hear the words—even if I don't really believe what she's saying is possible. "How?"

When I got home yesterday from my time with Topher, Alexis and Shelby were home. I let the whole saga spill out. Of course, Alexis immediately started Googling him to confirm his story. Then she went off on a rampage about men and their despicable ways. Shelby managed to drag her away—probably to tell her she was not exactly being helpful—and then we all got takeout and watched some shoot-em-up movie Alexis picked.

Shelby rubs my arm. "Have you talked to him today?"

"No." Even though he's texted me several times asking if we can talk. Apologizing. "I'm not sure what I would say."

"Well, do you have any other questions for him?" She nudges the spoon from my fingers and, despite my protest, eases away the ice cream carton before setting it on the coffee table.

Whatever. It was almost empty anyway. I pull the fleece blanket up to my chin. It's got a huge picture of

Colin Firth dressed as Mr. Darcy from *Pride & Prejudice* on it. Evie must have left it behind when she moved into her little bungalow a few streets over. "I don't know. Maybe."

"Like …?"

"Like … like was Frederick only pretending to be interested in you so we could double date and he'd have an excuse to be with us?" I whip out the words and cringe at how they sound. "I'm sorry, Shelbs. That you got caught up in my drama."

My friend laughs, and it's light and airy. "Don't worry about me. Frederick is handsome and charming, but I never really was interested in him like that."

Hmmm. "Good."

"Any other questions?" she prods.

Ugh, fine. "I thought princes could only marry royalty. Why would he start something he knew he couldn't finish and then claim to care about me?" It just doesn't seem like something Topher would do. Not the Topher I know, anyway.

"Lauren, I have never felt for a woman the way I feel about you."

But maybe that Topher isn't the real one after all.

Ow. My head hurts. Could be a permanent brain freeze. (Can you get one of those from eating an entire carton of ice cream in one sitting? Asking for a friend.)

"I don't know the answer to that." Shelby tugs on her earlobe as she focuses on me. "But look at Prince Harry and Meghan Markle. Maybe Topher's country doesn't have any requirements about who a monarch can marry."

"Maybe." I frown. Shaking my head, I reach back for the ice cream carton. But Shelby's sigh makes me stop, think. Ice cream won't fix this problem, will it? (I'm sorry, ice cream. I still love you. You just aren't what I need right now.)

"Shelbs, why does he have to be a prince? Why couldn't he be a regular Joe Schmoe? I could have handled anything else. But not … that."

She grabs a throw pillow and plays with the tassels. "Why not? I know your mom basically turned your lives into a reality show, but is that all that's at play here?"

"There's more." I've never told any of my friends about Danny. Sure, the basics—that I once upon a time dated rising musician and star Danny Haddox. But they don't know the rest. "Remember Danny? My ex?"

Shelby gives me an encouraging nod.

"After one of his shows, a fan of his sort of attacked me. She claimed it was an accident, but her push down two flights of stairs felt anything but."

My friend's eyes are wide as she gasps. "What? Were you okay?"

"I ended up in the hospital for a few days with a head injury, broken ribs, and two broken legs."

"Oh, Lauren. That's terrible."

"That's not the worst part." My lower lip trembles as I think back to those dark days. "My mother milked the accident for all it was worth. In fact, thanks to me, both she and Danny gained a ton of social media followers and exposure. While I lay in that bed, they both rose in popularity." I lean my head back against the couch and stare up at the still ceiling fan. "I'm sure my mother cared about me, in her own way, but Danny only pretended to give me sympathy. In reality, he showed up at the hospital and said he had a responsibility to his fans, that he couldn't stay behind to take care of me. He left the next day for his tour because the show must go on."

Shelby doesn't say another word, just curls up next to me and puts her head on my shoulder. Her hand finds mine under the blanket and she squeezes.

"After months of physical therapy, once my PT cleared me, I hopped a plane to San Diego, a place I'd always wanted to visit. And I promised myself I'd never again have anything to do with someone who would put their success and public image above the people he cared about."

Another squeeze. "I know Topher lied, but do you really think he's anything like Danny?"

"No." And that's the truth of it. Deep down, I feel like I *do* know Topher's heart. "And he didn't exactly lie either. It was my prompting that led him to be quiet. He told me that there was something big that would change my mind about him. But maybe I didn't want to know anything. I wanted to be ignorant, stick my head in the sand. Because that's what I do, right? I run away from my problems."

"It's your defense mechanism. We all have them." Her voice is quiet, almost guilt-ridden. What is Shelby's defense mechanism? "What are you really afraid of, friend?"

"I guess I'm worried that the second he steps back

into his real life—back into the spotlight—he'll become a different person. And I'll get my heart broken again."

For a while, the two of us just sit there, silent. That's not unusual with Shelby—she's definitely the quietest of us all. Or maybe the rest of us are just so loud that we tend to drown her out.

Finally, though, she speaks. "There's never a perfect solution for two people to be together. Real love requires compromise. And sometimes, sacrifice."

I glance over at her. She's got her eyes closed, lips pursed—and it makes me wonder if we're talking about me and Topher anymore. But what she's saying … it's got merit, as do most of the things that come from my sweet friend's heart.

"Essentially, you have to ask yourself if you want Topher more than you want a quiet life."

Ugh, she's right. Asking Topher to give up the crown for me isn't even an option. It's in his blood—and despite what he thinks he heard his dad say when he was younger, I know he will be an amazing king someday.

Which means either I sacrifice my own life—this one that I love, surrounded by my friends who are like family, in a bubble of my own making—and get over my fears of being in the public eye …

Or I let him go.

twelve

LET ME TELL YOU—THERE'S nothing more torturous than being in one of your best friend's weddings after going through a fresh breakup.

Of course, I'm deliriously happy for Evie, who is perfection itself as she twirls in her airy chiffon wedding dress, complete with a sweetheart neckline, beaded bodice, and sheer sleeves that travel to her wrists. Her brown hair is loose around her shoulders and she's decided to forgo a veil in favor of a rhinestone crystal and pearl headband. A lacy pattern of leaves and flowers decorates the sleeves of the dress, giving the illusion that Evie herself is a beautiful rose.

"Oh, Evs, you're simply gorgeous!" Kayla exclaims as she circles the bride. All five of us plus a photographer, Evie's mom, Connor's sister-in-law, Lola, and her two littles—who, despite chasing each other around the room like wild banshees, look freaking adorable in their flower girl dress and little ring bearer tux—are stuffed inside the bridal dressing room at the Japanese Friendship Garden. "If I was a crier, I'd be unloading buckets of tears right now."

"Good thing you're an unfeeling witch instead," Evie teases.

We all laugh as Evie sneaks an arm around Kayla's waist and lays her head against her matron of honor's shoulder. My heart squeezing, I pull out my phone and take a picture of the two of them—so completely happy, so content, with or without their men.

But the addition of Connor and Josh to their lives has taught them so much. Brought them so much joy.

And today, together, we celebrate that.

I flick at a tear that's threatening to ruin the makeup that Alexis expertly applied to my face just thirty minutes ago. Shelby's immediately at my elbow, thrusting a tissue into my hand and smiling sympathetically. Mumbling a thank you, I dab at the moisture under my eyes before stuffing the tissue into the pocket of my dress. (All dresses should have pockets. Just saying.)

Evie let us each choose our own style of bridesmaid's dress so long as they were floor-length and the same color—a deep burgundy that just screams Christmas. Shelby went for the simple halter, Alexis for a spaghetti-strapped, A-line number (side note: she's dyed her hair silver to match), and Kayla for a sexy V-neck dress with a slit up the front.

And me? I chose a keyhole dress with delicate straps that crisscross in the back. It's the most beautiful dress I've ever owned—and yet, I'm sure the sadness inside of me is emanating outward, dimming the glow I'm capable of.

Part of me can't help but wonder what Topher would think. With this dress, would I fit into his world? Do I even want to? Shelby's words from two days ago keep ping-ponging in my mind: *"You have to ask yourself if you want Topher more than you want a quiet life."*

Since the last day and a half have been filled with wedding festivities—manis and pedis, brunch, last-minute wedding favor assembling (Reese's Pieces in an adorable drawstring bag labeled with Evie and Connor's names and wedding date), the rehearsal and following dinner, and everything else in between—I haven't really had time to think about what I'm going to do.

But since Topher stopped texting me yesterday, I figure that maybe he's given up. Maybe he doesn't want this anymore. Sees that I'm more trouble than I'm worth.

Or maybe he's just giving me space.

Ugh. Why are relationships so confusing?

"All right, people." Kayla steps away from Evie and leans down to fluff the bottom ruffle of the bridal gown. "Looks like it's about time to get out there." She collects Evie's bouquet of wisteria and presses it into her hand.

At just that moment, the event coordinator for the garden knocks and pops her head inside. "It's about that time."

Kayla's eyes sparkle. "We know."

Alexis gives the smug matron of honor a shove and Evie's mom steps up to have a private word with her daughter. There's lots of cheek smushing and kissing and hugging and by the end, both of them are near tears. The only thing keeping them from crying is Kayla shouting at them to keep it together so they don't ruin their makeup.

My heart is raw watching them, and I turn away. Will that ever be my mom and me? Is reconciliation possible after so much time apart? Would my mother ever take time to have a private word with me, or would everything need to be recorded for "posterity"—aka, her audience?

Another knock sounds on the door and Evie's dad comes inside. Lucky for men, they don't have any such concern with makeup and I can tell in an instant that this big farm man has been bawling his eyes out. There's something so sweet about him as he sees his daughter and loses it again, and the three of them circle up and group hug.

Then Mr. Denmark is taking Evie by the arm and escorting her out the door. We follow. She and Connor wanted to wait until the ceremony to see each other— Evie's kind of traditional like that—and I sense her anticipation as she bounces on her heels in the hallway. Just outside these doors and down a short path, her groom awaits.

And so does her future.

We walk out the building's door and the cool early evening air greets us. Taking the short path, we arrive just at the edge of a copse of trees strung with bulb lights. Two sections of white chairs are filled with people—everyone from coworkers to friends and distant family members. Up front is an arch wrapped and adorned with vines and small white flowers.

The officiant is in the middle, and next to him, Connor is flanked by his guys. There's his best man and brother, Kevin, to his right, then Josh, Eric, and a few other colleagues and friends. Connor is looking handsome in his tux as he laughs and claps his brother on the shoulder.

While the coordinator arranges us in a line—Shelby first, then me, Alexis, Kayla, and Lola, who is helping walk the littlest attendants down the aisle—Alexis leans forward and whispers, "I will deny it if you ever repeat this, but Evie's found one of the good ones."

I turn in mock surprise. "So are you saying that not all men are pigs after all?"

A small smile flickers over her face. "I told you—I'll deny it." Then she straightens and studies her bouquet of lilies with the concentration of a grad student before a final exam.

"I agree with you, you know." And I do. Despite what's happened with Topher, I still believe in love. Still believe that there are good guys out there—even maybe that I found one.

I just don't know if he's right for *me*. If I fit into his life.

At the front of the gathering, a string quartet and keyboardist begin playing *Canon in D*. With a deep breath, I shake off all negative vibes and any thoughts of Topher. This is Evie's day. It's all about her.

Shelby heads on out and, just as always, there's a quiet elegance about her. She's classically beautiful—

and I think Eric knows it. I watch as his eyes follow her down. She doesn't seem to notice as she inclines her head and smiles at everyone else in the audience, but I can't help but wonder if the next wedding I attend will be for the two of them.

And, before I know it, it's my turn down the aisle and then I'm up front, watching Alexis, Kayla, Lola, and the kids come on down. A chuckle rises from the crowd when four-year-old Ellie tosses the flowers as high as she possibly can, one petal at a time. One-year-old Tommy starts picking them up—again, one petal at a time—and alternates between trying to eat them and putting them back in Ellie's basket. Meanwhile, Lola tries to urge them along and finally rolls her eyes and laughs like any tired mom would.

Then I feel a change in the air. A shift, like a breeze blowing one way and suddenly veering the other direction. The musicians end Pachelbel's song and a new song begins—and I've watched *Pride & Prejudice* enough times to know the scene it's from. Even though Evie largely despises the 2005 version and favors the one with Colin Firth as Mr. Darcy, she does concede the fact that the newer adaptation has an incredible musical score.

And right now, she's walking down the aisle to the song where Darcy and Elizabeth meet just before dawn —just before they make their wishes known for the final time. Just before the sun rises on their new life. The melody of the keyboard, accompanied by the strings, bends and builds to a crescendo while Evie floats down the aisle arm in arm with her father.

Her gaze is fixed firmly on Connor, and his on her. Both of them are crying and smiling like crazy. And when she finally reaches the front of the aisle, and her dad gives her away, Connor takes her by the hand and leads her to the arch, where we all watch the officiant welcome us and give a speech about love.

"Connor and Evie wish me to tell you a story, a story about a man and a woman who were both set on their own paths," he says. "Even though those paths looked like they'd always run parallel, eventually they crossed —and a literal earthquake shook them up."

The audience laughs and Evie and Connor grin at each other.

The officiant goes on telling Evie and Connor's love story, both the ups and the downs. But then, he says something that has me leaning forward, nearly toppling into Shelby before I catch myself. "There's something about love that makes you weak in all the best ways— able to be vulnerable, to admit that you need each other, to see that you are strongest when you're together, because a braided cord holds up much better than two individual strands on their own. But love also makes you strong, because a good partner challenges you to be a better version of yourself."

I inhale so sharply that Shelby peeks back at me, her eyebrows knitted in clear concern. I give a little shake of my head, but I can't help but think of Topher.

"Because talent like yours, when given freely and with the right motives, makes the world a better place. You can inspire people. You've certainly inspired me."

He's challenged me and I've challenged him, but it's always been in a gentle and authentic way.

"Love challenges us to face our deepest fears—and when we're there, on the edge of the watery cliff, ready to dive, it takes our hand and says, 'I'll jump too. You don't have to do this alone.'"

And now I'm full-on bawling, yanking the tissue from my pocket because I know—*know*—that I've found what Evie and Connor have. I just have to find the courage to reach for it.

I watch my friends recite their vows—"You're the most pulchritudinous thing I've ever seen, Webster, and I can't believe you're mine."—and then the officiant pronounces them husband and wife.

Their kiss is full of passion and heat, and Evie blushes when all the guys whoop and holler and we bridesmaids join. Music starts in and the groom sweeps his bride back down the aisle. We follow and there are happy hugs all around.

And all the while, I know what I need to do.

At the first possible opportunity, I sneak away, grab my phone, and send Topher a text asking him to come. I need him right now, and I'm not so strong or proud to hold that back.

It's true—I don't really understand how I'm going to weather the differences between Topher and me, but I know that I at least have to give us a chance. To talk. To work through it. To see what he says in return.

All I can do is hope and pray that Topher will see my fears, take my hand, and take the plunge to wherever the next cliff takes us.

Together.

The reception is more than half over. Photos flew by and dinner passed in a blur. We've been through toasts from Kevin and Kayla—both of whom ribbed Evie and Connor and had the whole place in stitches—as well as the cake cutting and first dance. (Connor and Evie swayed to Adele's "To Make You Feel My Love" and I nearly died at the mutual adoration in their eyes.)

Now, everyone is shimmying on the dance floor. The champagne is flowing freely and slices of cake sit half eaten on the abandoned (but beautifully attired) reception tables. Off to the right of the tables, a placid pond reflects the lights and the glow of heaters ringing the entire reception area. A DJ plays a nice mix of big band music—to which Josh and Kayla show off their swing dancing moves—and modern-day classics. He even sneaks an 'N Sync song in there and I'm teaching everyone the dance moves like it's the Electric Slide.

All in all, it's one of the best weddings I've ever been to. I'm surrounded by people I love—but not all of them. What will my own wedding day look like someday? As I watch Evie with her family, Connor with his, I can't help but ache with longing for my mom and sister. Will it ever be like this with us?

Maybe Mom has changed. Maybe I really was wrong to leave, to cut off contact with her. I was just so impulsive like always. So hurt. I wonder if now we could ever work through our issues in a more adult manner. You know. Just … talk. I'll never know if I don't go back. But could I ever be that brave?

I step off the dance floor and head for my seat, where there's a glass of water I've barely touched. Now that the reception's heavily underway, my bridesmaid's duties are basically over, so I can take a moment to relax.

But before I can sit down, there's a gentle touch on my elbow, along with a whispered, "Hello, love."

An involuntary flutter migrates up my arm and takes over my entire body. I turn and drink in the sight of Topher. He looks downright delicious in a crisp navy-blue suit that looks like it was custom made for him, drawn together and trimmed in all the right places, with a matching tie tucked inside the jacket. From the styled wave of his hair to his cognac leather shoes, the man's style is on point.

And every inch that of a prince.

I still have trouble seeing him that way, though. To me, he's just Topher. SuperThor.

Mine.

I hope.

Nibbling my lip, I drink him in. "You came."

"I always will." He steps back to take his turn assessing me. "Tiger, you look simply divine."

"Thank you."

Despite the raucous laughter ringing from the dance floor—where my friends are doing a ridiculous rendition of "YMCA"—Topher and I remain silent for several long moments before I realize he's waiting for me to lead the conversation. Which makes sense, since I'm the one who texted him.

I point down the pathway toward the rest of the garden, which is closed to the public for the wedding. "Want to take a walk?"

"Of course." He hesitates then offers me his elbow, which I take. His bicep flexes beneath my fingers.

We stroll away from the wedding, looping the pond until we eventually come upon a quaint wooden bridge stretching across a dry bed of rocks. The moon is large and clear above us, the stars skittering across the sky like a thousand jewels, some large, some small. I imagine I see one shooting from one point to the other, and I make a wish.

That this, right here, wouldn't be a dream.

That the feeling of his man beside me will last.

That somehow, I can overcome my fears to find a way for us to be together.

That he still wants that, too.

I drop my hand and, instantly cold, rub at my upper arms. "Topher—"

No more words come out before he whips off his jacket and sets it around my shoulders, and I know warmth once again. Not only that, but the scent I've missed so much the last few days—his—surrounds me, and I swallow hard to keep my self-control. I can't just go and kiss him like I want to. There's so much we need to discuss first.

"Lauren, I know you must have a thousand things to say, but I need to tell you something first."

Oh. "Okay."

He sighs and rubs a hand along his jaw, where his neat-and-tidy scruff has come in a bit more. Not quite a beard, but fuller than usual. "When you texted, I was just a few moments from leaving San Diego."

Not exactly what I'd hoped to hear. Him pining over me? Waiting forever for me? Forgive my romantic-notion-loving heart, but are THOSE things too much to ask? (Maybe. But still!)

I dip my gaze toward the rocks below the bridge, which have suddenly become very interesting. "I see."

"No, you don't." He takes a step closer. "The paparazzi found me yesterday."

"What? How?" My mind instantly drifts to Brittney. "Was it the girl from my spin class? Did she out you?" My stomach bottoms out as my eyes find his. "Do they know about me?"

He takes my hand in his, his thumb skimming my knuckles as he shakes his head. "No, love. These are a few paparazzi from my country. They've been looking for me for a while, since I haven't been seen and they knew a little something about my mental breakdown. Unfortunately, *that* made the news ... and you don't even want to know what they said about me."

Oh, Topher. "I'm sorry."

He waves me off. "I learned a long time ago not to pay attention to blatant lies. Regardless, they knew I'd be in Los Angeles for the charity ball in a few days, and someone on my staff tipped them off that I'd been here for some time. They found me yesterday and have been following me ever since."

"So you planned to just … leave?" I know the hurt is evident in my voice, but at the moment, I just don't care.

"I didn't want to, but Frederick and my family thought it would be best. My parents and sister will arrive in LA tomorrow and we already have a hotel suite reserved all week long. It made sense for me to head there a day early. So Fred and I packed and were about to head out when you texted me."

"I didn't mean to mess up your plans." My voice trembles. "So, wait. They found you—does that mean they followed you here?"

"Fred made sure to take back streets, so we don't think so. He's waiting in the parking lot to take me to Los Angeles after this."

"Oh. Well." I guess that's it, then. He has no desire to try to work things out between us. "Thank you for telling me."

"I felt you needed to have all the information to make a decision."

My pulse skitters at my throat. "A decision about what?"

"About whether …" He squeezes. "Whether you want to come with me. The hotel suite is large enough for you to have your own room. And there's the matter of the charity ball. I'd love for you to be my date. Though, of course, there will be cameras. Lots of them."

Coldness prickles along my fingertips and palm. "I …" Do I want that? Even knowing that the paparazzi might take my photo? Am I ready to be in the spotlight again?

He blinks down his nose at me, his expression guarded, unsure. "I know this life isn't for everyone. That you value your privacy because of what happened with your mum. And I'd never want to force it upon you."

I sigh. He deserves to know everything. "It's not just because of what happened with my mom. There's more to *that* story too." Then I proceed to tell him everything —Danny, the accident, the price of fame, the heartache of being left behind and being deemed less important than "duty."

We walk as I talk, and he listens patiently, stroking my hand the whole time.

Finally, we stop under the branches of a sprawling California oak. He lifts my hand and kisses it. "I'm sorry you had to go through all of that, love. But that man was a fool. If you give me a chance, I'll prove that it won't be like that with us. I will do everything I can to protect you."

"I know you say that now, but fame has a way of changing people and their priorities."

"But you're forgetting something, love. For better or worse, I've been famous all my life. If I was going to let them change me, don't you think it would have happened already?"

Hmm. He does have a point.

Topher continues. "As long as we're together, you will always be my priority. This I promise you."

I smile up at him. Moonbeams cut through the branches in shafts of light that illuminate his handsome face. "There you go speaking to me in 'N Sync lyrics again."

"Oh, you like that, do you?"

"You have no idea."

He chuckles softly, then cups my face with his free hand. "I mean it, Lauren. I may not know precisely what the future holds for us, but I do know that we are stronger together. You have taken a man deemed a snobbish prince and helped me realize that I need to be *with* the people, not over them. That the best way to serve them is to listen to them, not pretend I understand what they need because I read it in some blasted book."

His assessment of me makes me blush. "And you've got me thinking all sorts of thoughts about being brave," I say. "Seeing my family again, for starters. Maybe even pursuing my photography."

"Yeah?"

"Yeah."

"So … does that mean you'll come with me? Be my date? Meet my family? Give my father that big hug you promised?"

I smile at the memory. And when I look at this man —who is so much more than royalty to me—I know that I would give up everything I own to be with him.

"I'm not sure I can come with you tonight. I need to be here for Evie, and I've got work tomorrow and early Thursday. But I could drive up after that if that's all right?"

"It's more than all right. More than I dared hope for, really." He takes a step closer and my back is solid against the oak's massive trunk. Topher drops my hand and braces his arm just over my head. "And now, there are only a few things left to say." His lids droop and his face comes closer to mine, till all I see are his eyes, his regal brow.

Him.

"And what's that?"

"Lauren Smith—"

"Everly." If I'm going to move forward, I should do so as myself—the real me. Score another point for bravery.

"All right, then. Lauren Everly." His nose touches mine, and it's all I can do to keep my hands pinned at my side. "You're all I ever wanted."

Lyrics flood my brain as he leans in for a long, slow kiss before pulling away.

"You're all I ever needed," he continues, then goes back in, this kiss long and languid and knee buckling. My arms do the only thing they can and loop his neck as I lean back against the tree for support.

He drops a hand to my waist, drawing his finger along the fabric of my dress. "And I'm crazy for you."

Laughing, and breathless, I manage to pull together a coherent thought. "That's from a different song."

"You weren't supposed to catch that."

"Don't you know who you're talking to?" I tilt my head. "It's not fair. You know my weakness, but I don't know yours."

"I should think that would be quite obvious."

Me. He means me.

And that does it. I'm sunk.

Lifting an eyebrow, I run one hand down the length of his tie, then back up again before I pull him to me. He comes willingly and our lips connect again—but there's nothing slow or laid-back this time. Fire ignites in my bones, my blood, my skin. Topher is here, there, and everywhere, consuming me, his tongue tangoing with mine, giving me a glimpse of the passionate man behind the stoicism, behind the books.

And I gotta say—I like what I see.

As we kiss, my hands wrap deep into his hair, then drop to tour his shoulders, his chest. And when they untuck his shirt (those naughty little things have a mind of their own!) so my curious fingers can feel the washboard of his abs, the tautness of his waist, he groans at the contact and leans even further into me.

Our kisses become more heated and then we slow down again, a constant revving and cooling like we're at freaking NASCAR—but this race is a marathon and we're just rounding the first lap. I take his lower lip and gently nibble, then kiss along the outer rim of his mouth, taking extra care with the corners. His hitched breathing tells me that perhaps I've found another weakness. He tries to capture my lips once more and I dodge away, giggling.

"Tiger," he growls. Then he leans down again. "Two can play at that game, you know."

"Oh, really? Gonna use something you learned in your extensive reading?"

"There are some things that just come naturally."

A delicious shiver races up my spine as Topher angles his lips to touch the sensitive spot just below my ear. I inhale sharply at the contact, my fingers digging into his back as his mouth makes its way toward mine. But it's achingly slow, and I'm the Queen of Restraint as

I allow him to continue his ministrations, kissing my jaw, my cheek.

Then just as I think he's going to end my misery and take my abandoned lips again, he reverses course, back to my ear, pressing a firm kiss to the lobe. My body feels like it's been tossed in the cold ocean and I'm frozen with the shocking pleasure of it. All I can do is whimper and hang on for dear life to the handsomest flotation device a girl could ask for. His lips continue down my neck, etching a tattoo of his affection into my hot skin before dipping to my clavicle.

"All right." I'm not too proud to admit his kisses are driving me up a wall—or a tree, as it were—in the best way possible. "You're good. I'll give you that."

He pulls back and grins, his eyes glinting something dangerous in the starlight. "My dear, I play to win. Do you concede defeat?"

But I'm up for the challenge. "Never."

"You asked for it." In one swift move, Topher slides the jacket off my shoulders, letting it drop to the ground and pool around my feet. I'm leaning back against the tree once more, this time the bark boring into my skin— but the discomfort grounds me, keeps me here on earth when all I want to do is fly.

Then he takes my hand and starts planting kisses from the tips of my fingers allll the way up my arm, and I soar away again, headed straight for the heavens. When he gets to the skin on the underside of my upper arm and I sigh with pleasure, I know I've lost the battle.

But maybe it's not such a bad thing to surrender to a man like Topher James.

"Topher …"

"What?" He startles, straightens. "Was that too much?"

"No!" I shout, probably much too loudly.

He chuckles and runs a hand through his hair.

I tilt my head shyly and gnaw the inside of my lip. "Definitely not too much. It's perfect. You're perfect. And I'm … I'm all in with you."

He studies me for a long moment, his face a mask of concentration before speaking again. "I'm all in with you too."

Hearing those words is more than I can ask for. I may not know if Topher is the one I'll marry—if this will last—but right now, I can't imagine a world where he and I don't exist together. "What I was just going to say is that I think you win." I toss him a saucy smile. "This round, at least."

"So what you're saying is … there will be many rounds?" He wraps my arms around his waist.

"If I have my way? Many, many rounds."

"Good."

And then he takes my mouth, my body, captive again until I'm numb in my fingers and toes, craving his closeness, forgetting where I am, wanting, needing him—

"Your Royal Highness, we need to go."

Topher and I both freeze at Frederick's voice and I have to blink to clear away the kiss-induced fog in my brain. Without turning, Topher stoops to pick up his jacket and affixes it over my shoulders once more before pressing a chaste kiss to my lips. "Sorry, love." Then he takes my hand and escorts me back to the reception, where the noise and music feel like invaders to our private party.

My ears are still buzzing, my blood still pumping, and all I want is to stay by his side. "Maybe I can come with you now …"

"No, like you said, your friend needs you. And your loyalty is one of the things I love best about you." He dips and whispers in my ear. "I'll be waiting for you."

Then he melts into the forest again and I stand on the edge of the ring of tables, feeling like half of my soul just walked away.

thirteen

HOW DOES one go about meeting a king, queen, and princess for the first time?

Asking for a friend.

A really, really nervous friend who tried on a bazillion outfits this morning before her housemates told her that the best thing she could wear was her self-confidence.

So yeah, that friend is me. (Surprise!) And here I stand in the lobby of the most opulent hotel I've ever seen—we're talking Spanish tiles, gorgeous chandeliers, brass fixtures, marble floors, and furniture that looks much too expensive to sit on—twisting my hands as I wait for the elevator. A bellhop has already taken my bags so I don't even have something to hang on to. But I can't really expect any less from a Beverly Hills hotel like this one.

When the elevator opens, Frederick's there. He

flashes me a smile and waves me inside. "So glad you could join us, Lauren."

"Thanks." I step in and the smell of peppermint emanates around me. Even the elevator is fancy with rich carpeting and dark wood crown molding. Adjusting my long necklace, I lift my chin just slightly this way and that, using the elevator's three-hundred-and-sixty-degree mirrors to double-check that I didn't spill any coffee on my teal-green sweater during the drive up.

"Your trousers appear to be right-side-out this time." Freddy winks at me and I give him a shove before making sure he's right. Yep. My dark brown jeans fit me just the way God intended.

He uses a key card on the elevator sensor and then presses a button on the wall. The elevator begins its ascent to the top floor.

My lips twist into a frown and I fluff my hair, tugging on the ends. Maybe I should have taken time to get a haircut before meeting royalty. Sheesh. But after Evie's wedding sparkler sendoff, wherein Alexis's dress caught on fire thanks to one of Connor's very drunk cousins—don't worry, she's fine, just more convinced than ever that men are not only pigs, but idiots—and a full day of working and packing, there wasn't really the opportunity.

And now it's two days before Christmas and tomorrow's the ball and I've barely spoken to Topher and don't know what his parents know and don't know. What if they don't approve of me? What if his mom is one of those witchy queens I've seen in countless romcoms and fairy tales who hate the woman their son chooses? What if—

"They're going to love you. Don't worry your head." Though Frederick stands at attention, hands clasped in front of him, he manages a wink.

I fold my arms across my chest. "I didn't think even you wanted us together."

"That's not it. I just thought Topher needed to stop messing around and either reveal himself or let you go."

"Oh." Before I can come up with another reply, the elevator dings open to a large living room. Okay, then. I thought I'd at least have the length of a hallway to get myself together, but apparently not.

Freddy leads the way out the door and before I can react, I'm being tackled with a hug. But it's not the masculine hug I've been expecting. It's someone with a slight frame, slender arms, and a mass of curls that tickle my nose.

Someone who is squealing. "Oh my goodness, you're here!" That someone pulls back and I'm met with a face I know but don't know—she's got the same eyes and mouth as Topher, but instead of dark hair, hers is golden.

"Chloe?"

She laughs and it's like someone tapping a spoon against a thousand tinkling china cups. "Of course I'm Chloe! Who did you think? And you're Lauren. Sweet, amazing Lauren."

Um, okay. "I—"

"Give her some space, Princess." Freddy's voice teases, but not in the normal tone he uses when he jokes with Topher or me. There's a softness to it, and as I peek at him, I see a glowing admiration in his eyes—one directed at Topher's sister.

Oooooh. He may have flirted with Shelby, but it's clear Freddy's heart belongs elsewhere.

But Chloe doesn't seem to notice, just swats at Frederick and laughs again. "Nonsense. Lauren loves me. Don't you, Lauren?"

What's funny? I do. Seriously. This is not the welcome I expected. I had visions of me approaching the regal family seated on the edge of couches in large ball gowns and attempting to come up with diverting conversation that wouldn't label me a complete fraud.

Even the thought of it all sounds pretentious.

But Chloe, in her fashionable ripped jeans and casual off-the-shoulder black blouse, is the very opposite of pretentious. In fact, she feels like one of my girlfriends. She'd fit right in with Evie, Kayla, Alexis, Shelby, and me.

So I answer her the only way I can. Linking my arm through hers, I grin. "I do love you, Chloe."

"See, Frederick? I told you so." Then she tugs me through the living room. It's like a mini replica of the lobby, filled with fancy accents and decor that I'd never be able to afford to replace.

"So where *is* that brother of yours?" My voice carries thanks to the high ceilings.

"He's around here somewhere." Chloe's smile is

back as we pass several large windows showing off the Beverly Hills area, including the green edge of a park—likely as ritzy as the hotel itself.

I clear my throat at the reminder that I don't belong in this world. Not anymore. But for Topher, I'm here. "Good, because I need to kiss that gorgeous face of his ASAP."

Of course I say this as we emerge into the kitchen—where Topher is sitting at a table with two older people I can only assume are his parents. The man sports a full head of gray hair. He's trim and wearing slacks and a button-up shirt, a white-gray beard adorning his pale cheeks. The woman is all elegance and beauty, her nearly black hair done up in a bun, her flawless skin like porcelain. She's sporting a strand of pearls nestled against her lavender sweater.

There's a spread of tea, sandwiches, and salads on the table, and I've clearly interrupted lunch. As for the good prince, he freezes with a bite of lettuce on a fork suspended in midair, blinking at my voice—and the fact I just blurted out how badly I wanted to kiss him in front of his whole family.

Is there a laundry chute I can jump down? I could really use one right about now.

Chloe is instantly giggling next to me and I'm sure my face must be as red as the tomatoes in Topher's salad. Across from him, the man—whose back is so straight, it is a literal ninety-degree angle—lifts a gray eyebrow and turns his focus to Topher. "Your girlfriend, I presume?"

Girlfriend. We haven't put a label on what we are, but if Topher is calling me that …

Topher drops his fork to his plate and stands. "Yes." He looks between us, lips pressed together, and I angle my head. Why isn't he rushing to greet me? "Father, Mother, this is Lauren Everly. My girlfriend. Lauren, these are my parents, King Johnathan and Queen Charlotte of Kentonia."

So introductions are more formal in Kentonia. Ugh. Well, here goes nothing. I cross my feet and stoop low into a sort of half-dip, half-bow, my arms extended to my sides. "It's a pleasure to meet both of you."

When I attempt to stand again, my feet get tangled— and I fall on my rear.

"Lauren!" Now Topher dashes over and helps me up. "Are you all right? Bruised?"

I bury my face in his red T-shirt, breathing in his fragrance. "Maybe just my pride." Although my tail- bone doesn't feel great, I gotta say. I can't look at the king and queen. They must think I'm a complete Amer- ican buffoon. A clown.

"What …" Topher's lips twitch. "What was *that?*"

"A curtsy," I mumble.

And that's when all the laughter breaks loose, first from Topher, then Chloe, then the queen. But it's not malicious laughter. It's the teasing kind, and I know it when Topher tickles my sides and whispers, "You're adorable, you know that, right? That's another thing I love about you."

Next thing I know, Queen Charlotte is by my side,

swatting a cloth napkin at her son and pulling me into her arms. "Oh, my dear. That was most certainly *not* a curtsy."

I shake my head and grin. "That was the American version."

"Now, that I can believe." This from the king, who is still sitting there, looking as prim and proper as ever. He takes a sip of tea and then stands, extending a hand. "I believe this is how you greet one another in your country."

Chloe rolls her eyes. "And in ours too, Father."

"Yes, well."

Topher's right—the king *is* an older version of him, both in looks and personality. But though I feel suddenly intimidated by his large presence, the way he seems to take up the entire room's air, I made a promise—and I don't break those.

I step forward and throw my arms around King Johnathan like he's a long-lost friend. "This is another way we greet each other." The hug is quick and his arms never come around me, but I'm counting it all the same. "Thank you for having me."

Moving back to the shelter of Topher's arm, which he slides around my waist, I get the courage to glance back at the king. Is it my imagination or are the apples of his cheeks a bit reddened?

He blusters for a minute then gestures toward the table. "Join us for lunch, won't you?"

The table, which has eight chairs, is plenty large enough, so at my nod, Topher pulls out the chair next to his and I sit. The air between us all is quiet for a few moments as I make myself a plate of salad from the fixings.

Under the table, Topher squeezes my knee in encouragement. "We were just talking about the charity ball before you arrived."

I see what he's doing, and I'm thankful since I was positive the entire lunch was going to be spent grilling me for information about myself and my people. "It's for a local children's hospital, correct? How did your family get involved with that charity from all the way in Kentonia?"

The queen sips her tea, then sets it down. "We were here on business when Christopher was a child." She looks at him, as if waiting for something. Permission, maybe. When he nods, she continues. "He became gravely ill and needed an emergency appendectomy, and this particular hospital performed the procedure. The staff was wonderful, so compassionate, and they took beautiful care of our boy. After that, we became donors. And every year we are able, we travel here for the Christmas Eve charity ball, give a speech, raise awareness, that sort of thing."

"Christopher is actually giving the speech this year." Chloe's eyes dance as she picks up what looks like a blueberry scone. "Even though he hates public speaking."

"Really?" I glance up and find him watching me. "I didn't know that."

"I'm assuming there are a great many things you

don't know about him." The king's voice reverberates off the stainless-steel appliances in the large kitchen.

"Johnathan," the queen says.

"No, Charlotte, I must speak up. Our son informed us yesterday that there's a woman he's interested in and I know nothing about her. Forgive me for wanting to be sure she's not another Elizabeth, trying to pull him away from his duties."

"Father, I told you—"

"And I'm telling you, Christopher. I want to hear from Ms. Everly herself." His hawkish gaze finds me again. "So, why are you here?"

All four pairs of eyes are on me again, and I'm scorched. Chloe's are open, curious—not accusing, which is more than I can say for the king's. And while Topher's are apologetic, Queen Charlotte's are thoughtful. She clearly loves her son, but maybe she's willing to give me a chance.

I consider what Topher has told me about his father. Maybe this is his way of doing the same. He simply doesn't know how to show it—just like Topher, he's analytical. He won't understand sentiment. Me saying I love Topher won't sway him. (Aaaaaand just thinking those words does something to my insides, because if they're not true yet, I'm pretty sure they will be soon.)

Taking a deep breath, I look King Johnathan straight in the eyes. "I'm here because I believe your son will be the best darn king Kentonia has ever seen. No offense to you, of course."

The king places his elbows on the table and folds his hands together. "Well, I happen to agree with you."

Beside me, Topher coughs. I turn to catch a glimpse of emotion in his eyes—and why not? His father just admitted that the lie Topher believed all these years is, in fact, a lie. It's my turn to squeeze his knee in solidarity.

"But"—the king continues—"what does that have to do with you being here? He will be a great king with or without you."

"That's where you're wrong, Father." My man speaks up, his voice solid, sure. "Lauren makes me better, just like Mother makes you better. They soften us and pull us from our books into reality."

I glance at the queen, who dabs at the corner of her shining eyes with a napkin. "Hear, hear."

King Johnathan's hard glare seems to melt along the edges when he looks at his queen. Then he nods at me. "Well, then. You are very welcome."

"Thank you." I take a bite of my salad, and chicken and feta over lettuce have never tasted so delectable and refined before.

"Now that we have that out of the way, I'm dying to know." Chloe leans forward. "Lauren, what does your gown look like for the ball?"

"Oh, well, I just brought the bridesmaid dress I wore earlier this week to a friend's wedding."

But then, a terrible thought occurs. I choke and reach for my water.

Because I'm fairly certain that gown is still hanging in my closet. No, no, no! I just knew I'd forget something important. This is what happens when Impulsive Lauren tries to actually make plans.

"I know that look," Chloe says. "And it means shopping! Oh, Mother, can we go this afternoon?"

"I don't see why not."

"Oh. Um." I don't have the funds to pay for something like that.

But Topher must sense my dismay, because he leans over and whispers, "It's on me, love. Buy whatever you want."

I arch an eyebrow and hiss back at him, "You know I won't take advantage of people."

"I'm not people. And you can repay me later, when you kiss this gorgeous face of mine."

With his wink, we're back in familiar territory and I poke him in the side, grinning. It doesn't matter that he's royalty or that I made a fool of myself in front of Kentonia's most famous people or that he's rich and we don't come from the same world.

He's just Topher and I'm just Lauren.

I'm letting go and just feeling.

And right now, I feel the love.

After the wonderful afternoon and evening I just spent with Topher's family, I shouldn't be considering possibly ruining it with a text.

Yet here I lie in the hotel bed, my phone clutched in my hand. Thanks to my open curtain, tonight's large moon spills light onto the floor of my private room within the presidential suite. The street is twenty stories down, yet I can hear the distant traffic of Beverly Hills. They say New York is the city that never sleeps, but I think the same can apply to Los Angeles.

And though I should be asleep—my clock says it's past one and everyone said good night over an hour ago—I've got too full a heart at the moment.

Too full a mind.

Shopping with Chloe and Charlotte—she told me to drop the "queen" bit when we're in private—was probably no big deal to them. But it was everything to me.

We spent the day on Rodeo Drive, with me modeling dress after dress until we settled on the perfect one: an emerald-colored gown with one shoulder and pleats that give the dress a really cool waterfall effect from the waistline to the ground. The dress's train sweeps the floor, covering the strappy silver heels that the women insisted I also purchase. The whole ensemble makes me feel not like a woman who falls over when she curtsies, but one who is elegant and poised.

Ha. We'll see if I fool anyone.

After we shopped, we hit a bakery for coffee (Chloe's addiction) and cupcakes (Charlotte's addiction) and had a lovely time as they asked me about myself ... then about Topher and me. It felt a bit strange to be so open with virtual strangers, but they were so welcoming and friendly that I couldn't help myself.

I fully braced myself to be attacked by the paparazzi, but it never happened. Maybe with so many celebrities in the area, the queen and princess of a small country aren't as large a draw. Either way, it was nice to feel like they were just normal people.

Well, other than the protection detail trailing us and the cars with tinted windows and the fact they spent hundreds on clothing. (Or was it thousands? Chloe wouldn't let me see the receipts.)

When we got back to the hotel, Chloe busted out the cards and we all played poker. And guess what? Queen Charlotte of Kentonia is a hilarious card shark. Watching them tease each other and laugh—even the king— reminded me of what I've been missing.

Thus … the text I'm contemplating sending.

I've already got it typed out. Have changed it a thousand times. Deleted it. Rewritten it.

It's time to just send the darn thing.

Once I read it one more time.

Hey Sam. It's me. You know … the sister who hasn't visited home in a long time and you rarely hear from. Yeah. So, some stuff has happened recently that's made me extra sad about how things have been for the last five years.

And I know that's my fault. I know it. I was running away from my feelings. Running away from Mom and the lifestyle she forced us to live. After Danny … well, I just had to get away.

But I was wrong, Sis. And I'm so sorry for all the ways I've failed you. I'm sorry you got caught in the cross fire. Because you were innocent in all of this. I just didn't know how to have a relationship with you too. I told myself it was easier to get away.

Like I said. I was wrong.

So … are you open to seeing me again? I'd like to come to

visit for New Year's if you and Mom are available and want to see me too.

I know it will probably take a really long time for you to forgive me. I'm prepared to do whatever it takes to show you that I'm here … and this time, I won't abandon you.

I'm so sorry. And I love you.

Lauren

Taking a breath, I hit Send. I don't expect to hear anything from her anytime soon—or ever, if I'm honest. So I plug my phone in on the side table then lie back against the extravagant pillows and close my eyes. Time for sleep.

But thirty minutes later, it's eluding me. All I can do is check my phone every five minutes to see if Samantha has returned my message. Which is dumb, because it's like four-something in the morning on the East Coast.

I need to get out of this room. Away from my phone.

I need a distraction.

I need Topher.

Slipping from my covers, I ease open my bedroom door. It emits a squeak and I wince. My feet are cold against the wood floors as I patter down the hallway. I feel like a teenager sneaking around, especially when I breathlessly skitter past Topher's parents' room.

When I reach his door, I don't even hesitate to open it, step inside the room, and shut the door again behind me. And I don't know why the sight in front of me should surprise me, but it does. Topher's side table light is on and he's sitting up in bed, reading.

Shirtless.

Of course he's shirtless. He's about to go to sleep.

Oh gosh, is he also … pantless? I swallow hard as the sudden thought careens into my tired brain.

He closes his book and blinks at me, before tilting his head and chuckling. "You going to come any closer?"

"Undecided." I twirl my finger in his direction. "What kind of clothing situation are we dealing with here?"

"If you're asking if I sleep in the nude, the answer is no." He winks. "Not tonight, anyway."

"A-and, um, what exactly *do* you sleep in?" My bare legs—yes, I sleep in shorts no matter how cold it is—are now covered in gooseflesh and I'm crossing my arms over my old track and field T-shirt to try to warm up.

Topher tosses back the comforter on the spot next to him and pats the mattress. "Why don't you come and find out?" He lifts a suggestive brow. At my clear hesitation, he shakes his head, smiles. "I'm wearing trousers, Lauren."

"Good." I scamper over and jump into the bed, yanking the comforter back over my legs. The heat from the blanket—and fine, Topher too—warms me right up. "I just didn't want you to think I came here for … that."

"Too bad."

"Topher." I hit his arm. "Stop it."

"Why? It's so fun riling you up." Then he's tickling my sides and I'm trying not to laugh or squeal too loudly because the last thing I want is for someone to barge in here thinking the prince of Kentonia is being attacked.

Before I know it, we're a tangle of legs and arms, and he's got me pinned. Topher lowers himself to me and kisses my neck where he knows I like it—the delightful rogue. Then he collapses back onto the bed.

I curl up beside him, resting my head in the crook of his arm, placing one hand on his bare chest, running my fingers through the short hair there—and it's just as soft as I imagined it. "I like seeing you like this."

"Half naked?"

"No!" Laughing, I pinch his side. And thanks to his muscles, I come away with nothing but skin. It's disgusting how fit he is. A girl who likes ice cream as much as I do could get a complex or something. "Relaxed. When I first met you, you were kind of a hard nose."

"Who, me?" His fingers brush my temple, my ear, with a gentle caress. Then he sighs. "I've told you. I was trying to hold you at arm's length."

"Just me? Or were you like that with everyone?"

"Maybe not Chloe or Fred. But most everyone else." His heart beats steady beneath my fingers as I splay my palm over his chest. "My mum actually said something similar to me earlier tonight. That I'm different with you around. She really likes you, you know."

My toes flex against the top of his foot. "I really like her too."

"And Father … well, I think you won him over with that hug, to be honest."

"Shocked him is more like it."

"We all need a good shocking now and again." He squeezes me.

We lie like that for a while, our breaths mingling together as we sink into the foam mattress. I don't know what tomorrow will hold—the cameras, the questions—but here, in this room, we are all that exist.

"Much as I love your company, was there something on your mind? If not, that's completely all right. I'm having the best time simply holding you."

"And I'm having the best time being held." I pause. "I texted my sister tonight." I tell him everything—all the feelings that being around his family has wrought, all the ways my sorrow has been crashing in, all the longing I feel to reconnect with my roots. With my people.

"Not that my friends aren't my people, but they're all moving on. First Kayla and Evie, and Shelby and Alexis will eventually join them. They'll find good guys and get married and have babies and will have their own lives. We will always be friends, of course, but their priorities will change."

Topher is silent for a moment before speaking again. "And you? Do you hope to get married and have babies and your own life someday?"

I shift back a bit so I can look up into his eyes. "Topher." My hand finds his cheek. "I wouldn't be in Los Angeles right now if I didn't. I'm not playing around here. I … I see a future with you. And that's scary, because it means having to face the thing that I'm most afraid of."

"I'm not playing around either, love." His fingers find my stomach as his eyes devour me with careful study. He traces a figure eight around my belly button, his touch sending my whole body spiraling into a fiery infinity. "You have me believing that true happiness is possible."

Gah. This man.

I snuggle into him and the last thought I have before peace—and sleep—overtakes me is that he's got me believing the same thing.

fourteen

· · ·

THERE'S no grand staircase in this fairy tale, but I don't need one.

The second I step into the suite's living room the next night—Christmas Eve—Topher's eyes travel from his phone to me, and his jaw slackens.

We're all alone except for Frederick, who is hiding in some other room at the moment. Topher's family went on ahead to the charity ball about a half-hour ago, after Chloe helped me do my hair and makeup.

"There," she said, backing away with the blusher and giving a nod. "You look like a real princess now."

And that's how Topher's making me feel as he drops the phone on the coffee table, stands, and moves across the room faster than a boy band groupie who just spotted Justin Timberlake in a crowd.

"Lauren ..." That's all he says as he takes my hand and spins me. The gown flares out at the bottom, just like Chloe said it would. "You are magnificent. Lovely. Handcrafted perfection."

"Go on, Encyclopedia Britannica." I wink and smile up at him. "You don't look so bad yourself." That's basically the understatement of the century. I thought the man wore a suit well—but a tux? Daaaaang. He's debonair and approachable all at once. Handsome, but once again, not full of himself.

And this man—this prince—is looking at *me* like I'm more than the opening act. He's looking at me like I'm the main event.

Not sure I'm getting over that one any time soon.

"All the women at the ball are going to be salivating over *you*," I say. Then I move my pointer finger side to side. "Spin."

My favorite smile smooths over his face like buttah as Mr. Dimple makes a triumphant return. "Is this just an excuse to gain a look at my backside?"

Uh, no comment. "You made *me* spin. I think I deserve the same courtesy." I place a hand on my hip. "I know you're a prince and not used to being told what to do, but—"

He sneaks a quick kiss, surprising me with his impulsivity. Maybe I've taught him a thing or two after all. "You may tell me anything you wish, love. I am at your beck and call."

"I'm going to remember you said that later."

"I hope you do." Then, before I can grab him and mess up his hair with a little kissing action, he spreads his arms wide and begins to spin.

Slow. Like molasses dripping off the edge of a spoon.

And my, oh my, do I ever enjoy the show.

When he's facing me again, a wicked grin on his face, I know he's caught me staring, but I can't help it. I'm fairly convinced I'll be having him spin for me like this at least once a day, from now until we're both ninety and wrinkled and I still think his butt is cute.

Whoa, Tiger. Slow your roll. Topher and I haven't even said "I love you" yet. I probably shouldn't be imagining us in our dotage.

And yet … I do.

He gives me another kiss, this one slower and deep, then sighs against my mouth. "We should probably be going."

"Aw, but you said you're at my beck and call." I pout.

Tapping me on the nose, Topher squeezes my waist before stepping away. "Later, Tiger."

"I'm holding you to it." I walk to the side table and pick up the clasp purse I set there earlier. "I suppose we wouldn't want the star guest to be late, now would we?"

He groans. "Don't remind me." We hit the elevator button and wait for the doors to open. "Thank you for coming tonight. How do you feel about all of it?"

"Honestly? Nervous." Because even though I'm sure about him, there's still the whole stepping back into the public eye thing.

Taking my hand, Topher kisses it. "I'll be right beside you the whole time."

"Promise?"

"Of course." A pause. "You're not the only one who's nervous."

"You're going to do great. Is your speech all prepared?"

The elevator dings open and we step inside. Like a stealthy cat—always lurking, always there—Freddy joins us without a word.

"It is." Topher reaches into the pocket of his jacket and pulls out a folded paper, which he hands to me. "You're welcome to read it if you like."

"I *would* like."

And that's how I occupy my time once we're loaded into the back of the limo Freddy leads us to. As I read about Topher's experience as a child, how it shaped him and his view of those in service—how it inspired him to want to be the same kind of person, who helps others— tears rush to my eyes. When I finish, I refold the note and hand it back to Topher.

"What did you think?"

"It's blasted brilliant, that's what." I cry-laugh and yank a tissue from a box in the console between us, dabbing carefully at my eyes so Chloe's work doesn't go down the drain. "You struck the perfect blend of personal, inspirational, and logical."

He takes my hand in his. "That's all you, love."

"It's true," Freddy pipes up from his seat closer to the front of the limo. "I saw an earlier draft of the thing a few weeks ago, and it was pure rubbish."

I giggle as Topher tosses the tissue box at Freddy, who shields his face and laughs.

"Thanks a lot, mate."

"It was all intellectual nonsense."

"He's got me there." Topher looks down at me, mirth in his eyes. "I didn't know how to connect with my people—any group of people, really. You showed me how."

His kisses are liquid joy on my lips.

Freddy clears his throat. "Much as I hate to break up this love fest, we're here, Your Royal Highness."

Topher leans his head back against the seat. "I've told you not to call me that in private."

"Force of habit." The car rolls to a halt. "Nevertheless."

And suddenly, a whole swarm of bees takes flight inside my stomach. Because I can hear them—the clicking of the cameras. The shouts of people. And though the windows are tinted, I imagine I can see the bright lights too.

I sit back and force a breath into my lungs, which are suddenly tight. Sweat beads on my temple and heat races up my spine—not the good kind that Topher elicits, but the kind you get when you've got a fever or are about to throw up. I place a fist against my stomach.

Topher's looking over his speech again and doesn't seem to notice my reaction.

You can do this, Lauren. You have *to do this.*

"Ready, love?" He turns to me as he tucks the paper back inside his jacket.

"You sure we can't just go back to the hotel?" The tease I intended comes out rather strangled. "Or let's go get ice cream. Doesn't ice cream sound good?"

His nose wrinkles. "But my family's waiting inside. I

have to give a speech." Guess he doesn't get the joke—though if he took me up on it, I'd be all over a scoop of cookie dough right about now.

"I was just kidding."

But he continues as if he doesn't hear me. "People are counting on me. It's my duty to be here."

I flinch at the way his words sound almost exactly like what Danny said to me before he left to go on tour five years ago.

Must be strong. Must be brave. "I know that. It's fine. Let's go."

"Good, then." He swivels his gaze back to the door. He's focusing on what's ahead. Probably practicing his speech in his head again, and I'm distracting him from what he's got to do.

All right. It's now or never.

And never isn't an option.

Freddy exits first, then holds the door for us. The sound rushes in and my ears feel like cotton's been stuffed inside. I'm positive that breathing is about to become impossible. I want to cry, but I'm afraid that if I start, I won't be able to stop.

But as I'm about to grab Topher, tell him what I'm feeling, he is outside the vehicle. And I have to join him —have to prove to him, to myself, that I can step back into the public eye with my head held high.

Just when I'm sure I'll collapse, his hand reaches back for me and I grasp it. Hard. Because he's got me. He said he would be by my side the whole time, and he meant it. When he pulls me out, the cold air forces my breaths, cools me down just a tad. I sigh with relief.

But then there's the red carpet ahead. It's longer than I thought, and lined with people. This charity event must attract a lot of big names to warrant such a crowd and so much media, whose cameras are pointed in our direction. I hear shouts of "Prince Christopher!" and try my best to tune them out.

We take a step but my legs freeze and I dig my heels into the carpet. Topher tugs on my hand but he must notice my reticence, because his eyes settle back on me. "Lauren?" When I don't answer, he continues. "Come on." He squeezes my hand. "It'll all be over soon. There's nothing to worry about. Just smile and you're sure to dazzle them."

"Just smile, Lauren. No matter what you feel, just smile." My mother's words echo in my brain.

"Smile, babe." Danny hovers over me in my hospital bed, his phone flipped to selfie mode. "That fan did us a favor when she pushed you. Now we're both going to be famous."

I know Topher isn't trying to be callous, but it's hard to tell the difference when the effect is the same.

"I just need a moment."

The lines crease between his eyes and he looks back and forth between me and the media, who are screaming his name even more fervently. "I'll go talk to them and you can come when you're ready. How's that?"

How's that? What happened to him never leaving me?

"Sure," I manage.

He drops my hand—and I'm bereft. Standing there on the sidewalk like an idiot. Alone.

People look at me, curiosity in their expression, cameras pointed my way.

Maybe I should just duck back inside the limo, get my bearings. Or sneak off for that ice cream after all.

I pivot—but the stretched vehicle is already gone. In its place is an expensive blue sports car with a female passenger glaring up at me, clearly annoyed that I haven't moved to allow her a private exit.

In fact, there's an entire line of cars stretching down the road, waiting for Lauren Everly to get her butt in gear.

I have no choice.

Summoning every ounce of courage I have, I straighten my shoulders and toss on that old familiar so-fake-I-wanna-puke grin before waltzing down the red carpet. I pass Topher where he chats with some camerapeople, as if he doesn't have a care in the world.

Maybe he doesn't, especially as it concerns me.

The cameras click and whirr. People ask me questions and I evade them. Topher catches me and grabs my hand again. Because now, it's convenient.

Nu-uh.

When we finally reach the inside of the charity ballroom—a lavish place decorated in shimmery golds and reds, with lights and elegant frosted Christmas trees and guests dressed in the latest designer wear—I drop the smile. And his hand. "Happy?"

"Tiger ..."

"Don't you *Tiger* me." I point back at the door. "*That* was one of the worst experiences of my life. I nearly had a panic attack, Topher, and you didn't care one bit!"

"What?" He reaches for me again. "Love, I didn't know."

"That's because you weren't listening. Your precious responsibility was more important to you than I was." Yanking away, I spit the words like they're venom, poisoning me from the inside out. "You promised to protect me. And then you left me behind."

"I just didn't know what to do. The media were clamoring for an interview and you seemed fine one minute and then—"

"Yeah, well, sorry my past triggered some deep-seated anxiety at a time when it was unacceptable for you."

I don't even recognize my voice. Fear is clearly masquerading as anger, but right now, it's easier to grasp at the latter.

Because what I worried about … it came true.

Topher was different in public than he was in private. And he asked me to be too. He asked me to change who I was, what I was feeling, and put on an act.

To be inauthentic.

Just like my mom and Danny always did.

Maybe I've had it all backward. Maybe *this* is real life and our time alone—singing 'N Sync while decorating a tree, hiking a new trail to both of us, kissing in a garden, making promises of protection—is what's fake.

"Excuse me, Prince Christopher?" A woman in a stunning black dress taps him on the shoulder, a tape recorder in her hand. "Jessica McDonald with *Royal News Today*. Do you mind answering a few questions for me?"

His mouth opens, closes, and he looks at me again, pleading and questions in his eyes.

"Go on." My voice is gentler now, resigned. "Your duty awaits." And I won't keep him from it.

"Lauren …"

"No, really. We can talk about this later. Proceed, Prince Christopher." His formal name and title leave a bitter taste in my mouth.

Despite the pressing together of his lips, he returns his focus to Jessica and begins answering her questions.

And I slink away, leaving my heart smashed on the dance floor before the first song has even begun.

How can a hotel have a bathroom that's larger than Alexis's whole house?

I contemplate this all-important question of the universe while stretched out on one of said bathroom's couches. (There are five. Yes, five.) In this reclined position, my dress has lost all its poofiness and pizzazz—or maybe that's just me.

Women who are here to, you know, actually use the restroom look at me then dart their eyes away before heading into their stalls. Not sure if I disgust them with my smudged mascara and box of half-used tissues on my lap or just scare them. Or maybe worse.

Maybe I ignite their pity.

Ugh. I pull my phone from my purse again but still

there's nothing from Shelby. I texted her thirty minutes ago to see if she could come to get me. Of course, she's a few hours away in San Diego, but still. I can sit here all night if it means not having to face Topher again.

I thumb away text notifications from him and his pleading for me to come back and talk—and then I pause. There's one from Samantha. My finger hovers over the message, but no. If she's refusing to see me or says something equally emotionally damaging, I simply don't have the bandwidth to deal with it right now.

Tears begin leaking down my cheeks again and I yank another tissue from the box.

"Oh, my dear."

Glancing up, my eyes widen at the sight of the queen of Kentonia, radiant in a bright red gown with elegant cap sleeves and elbow-length gloves and standing in the white-tiled bathroom. She motions to her female body-guard, who clears the whole bathroom of people and then stands guard at the door.

Maybe she's here to ream me out for hurting her son and doesn't want an audience. I can't stand the idea of disappointing her. I sit up so she can take the seat next to me if she wants. "Queen Charlotte—"

"Charlotte, remember?" She eases herself gracefully beside me. "Christopher told me you're in here. He begged me to check on you. The poor boy is pacing around outside mumbling to himself. I suspect he was nearly about to break a thousand rules of etiquette and barge inside himself when I came upon him."

I sniff. "Really?" Part of me assumed that when I didn't answer his texts, he would have shrugged off my exit and slipped on a facade as he schmoozed and fulfilled his duties. But showing his emotions so openly and in such a wild way? "That's not all that dignified."

Oops. I just insulted her son. But the twinkle in her eye and quirk of her lips are evidence she's not offended. "Not at all. That's what love does to a person."

"Love?" My tone betrays my hope. "I mean, I thought maybe he felt the same way about me as I do about him, but …" Too late, I realize what I've said.

What I've admitted.

Her quirk widens to a grin. "I suspected as much."

Elation fills my chest, but reality deflates it again. I fist the tissue in my hand. "He didn't show his love very well tonight."

"In what way?"

I run my tongue along my upper teeth. What will the queen think of me if I tell her about my past? But I do it anyway. Then, "He knew how difficult it would be for me to give up my privacy, and yet, he left me on that red carpet because my need for a moment didn't align with his plans. He forged ahead and nothing was stopping him—not even my feelings." Rubbing my arms against a sudden prickling, I frown. "Not even his promises."

"My dear, there's something you must understand about the Huntington men. They carry the weight of the world on their shoulders, and their natural inclination is to figure out the best way of tackling that world and bringing it under submission. When they think they know it, they storm forward, swords lifted." She pats my hand. "And occasionally, those they love get a bit trampled in the charge."

"I can see that." I sigh. "Fame has a way of ruining everything." Especially my dreams.

"My dear, fame has nothing to do with it."

"How can it not?" I scrunch my nose at her. An air freshener somewhere in the restroom beeps and dispenses a fresh whiff of lemony scent.

"Of course, fame is part of our life. There are some concessions you'd have to make if you were to ever join the royal family—believe me, I did. I was a commoner too, you know."

"Really? Topher never told me that."

"Because he truly doesn't care about status or titles. He wants to do a good job leading his people, but if I know my son, he would have been the same person if he'd been born to a laboring family. And you, I suspect, would have still fallen in love with him. Am I right?"

I nod. "I didn't know he was a prince when I started to care about him."

"Every life will have its challenges. Your own is not free of them, I imagine."

She's right in that respect. "No."

"Famous or not, life is all about keeping the right perspective." The queen takes a fresh tissue from the box, tilts my face, and begins to blot my tears away like a real mother would.

My chin trembles.

"In a relationship, you must not let any outside opinions matter more than that of the one you're with. You must stay committed to being honest with each other, honest with yourself. And you must learn to forgive, because your partner will not be perfect, just as you are not perfect."

She pulls back, looks my face over again, and nods. Then she tosses the tissue to the side and takes my hands in hers, leaning forward in earnest. "And if you can do those things, then you can survive anything life throws at you. For richer or poorer. In sickness and in health. For better ..." She squeezes. "Or worse."

She's right. Totally. Completely.

If I really love Topher, then I need to realize he's not going to do everything right. And neither will I. If we want to have a healthy relationship, then I can't run away and refuse to talk every time something bothers me.

And I can't let one incident—one fight—define our whole relationship or be a sign that we shouldn't be together.

Because he's not my mom. He's not Danny.

He's both Topher *and* Prince Christopher.

And I love all parts of him—because they make up the essence of who he is.

I know Charlotte just cleaned me up but I can't help the fresh tears that start falling again. They only amplify when she pulls me into her arms and lets me cry all over her beautiful ball gown.

Finally, my tears are spent and I mumble an apology as I pull back.

She just smiles and waves another tissue in the air. "Nonsense. Do you know how many times Chloe has left mascara stains on my clothing after a good cry?"

That makes me laugh despite my now stuffy nose.

Together we stand and I get a glimpse of myself in the mirror. "Oh, man." It's like a train wreck meeting a bomb went off on my face—the Hot Mess Express is baaaaack, folks.

Charlotte takes my shoulders from behind and winks. Then she directs her attention to the bodyguard. "Ring Chloe, please. We need her."

A few minutes later, the princess whirls into the bathroom, lovely in a deep blue mermaid-style dress, her golden curls wild and free around her shoulders. "What is it—" She gets one look at me and her eyes widen. "Oh, dear."

"I presume you came prepared?" The queen arches an eyebrow.

"Of course. Who do you think I am, an amateur?" With a grin, Chloe opens her purse and yanks out an emergency supply of makeup. Then, through some sort of magical voodoo powers, she freshens me up so well I can't see a trace of the tears other than the slight red in my eyes, which she unfortunately can't do anything about.

I yank her into a hug. "Thank you, Chloe."

"I just hope you'll forgive my idiot brother for whatever he's done to make you this upset." She rolls her eyes. "He sometimes thinks a little too hard with his head instead of his heart."

"True." I press my lips together. "And I hope he forgives me for leaving and hiding out again. It's a bad habit that I'm trying to break."

"We all have those, now don't we?" A brief flash of

something befalls Chloe's gaze, but it's gone before I can analyze it.

Arm in arm, the two of us stroll past the bodyguard—Queen Charlotte on our heels—and out the bathroom door, where there's a line of impatient women. Oops. I forgot that we kind of took over the main restroom for the event, which is now in full swing.

A live orchestra plays on stage, guests dance, and waiters with platters full of appetizers and beverages circle the room.

As we emerge into the ballroom, a few photographers find us. "Queen Charlotte, Princess Chloe! Who is that with you?"

My heart leapfrogs into my throat, but the queen steps up beside me and joins my free arm with hers. "Lauren is family."

We pose and smile, but I know mine is wavering at the queen's kind words.

Because while family *is* the people you choose, it's also the people who have your heart—even when you're apart from them.

And right now, I need to find Topher and tell him how I feel before I burst.

Chloe scampers away when she sees someone she recognizes, and Charlotte is pulled into a conversation with an old friend, leaving me alone to scan the crowded ballroom on my tiptoes. But I might as well be looking for a golden ticket in a sea of candy bars.

Then, just as I'm about to lose all hope, one song ends—and the orchestra swaps its classic Christmas playlist for something quite different.

And so begin the opening measures of a song that I know better than the fine hairs between my eyebrows that constantly need tweezing. My eyes pivot to the stage, where a well-dressed man with a microphone is lit by a spotlight. His jacket is stripped away, his tie is loose, and his once-styled hair is tousled.

And he's looking at me like I'm the reason.

I'm a magnet and the people around me are water droplets, scattering and leaving me alone on the dance floor. But I don't really care about them, because the man in front of me is a magnet too, drawing me to him.

And when he opens his mouth to croon the lyrics to "I Want You Back," I can't help the giggle that erupts. It's the sound of pure joy spilling out of me, so opposite from the tears of minutes ago.

Topher's got all the right moves, and I can hear the women in the crowd swooning, can imagine them fanning themselves much like I did at the 'N Sync reunion concert three weeks ago.

But Christopher Alexander James Huntington is sexier than any of the Fab Five (sorry, boys, but it's true).

Because he's singing—and dancing—to me. For me. No way would this man be making a fool of himself in front of this important crowd if he didn't love me back.

I lift the skirt of my dress and race through the crowd, finding the stairs on the edge of the stage and taking them as quickly as my heels will allow. Then I take another mic from a stand and join him in singing the final chorus.

This is utterly ridiculous, especially at a dignified venue like this, but at the moment, I simply don't care.

We aren't a prince and a maybe-someday princess.

We are Topher and Lauren.

And when the song ends and we hand our mics to some poor stagehand who was probably bribed to allow this whole thing to occur, I step toward my future and embrace him hard.

"I'm sorry for running and hiding," I breathe into his shoulder.

"I'm sorry for giving you a reason to." He kisses my temple, my cheek, my nose. "If it's not completely obvious by now, Lauren Everly, I love you. You saved me, and I don't just mean when you kept me from being smashed by that car."

"I love you too, SuperThor." We laugh at my stupid nickname for him. "And together, I believe we really can do anything."

"Anything?" He lifts a hopeful brow. "Maybe even one day … run a country?"

"Maybe even that."

Then he kisses me, and I hear the awwwws start in. But I don't care about the watching eyes or what the crowd is thinking. Don't care about the pictures they're taking or the way the media might skew things.

I know the truth.

And that—plus this man in my arms—is all that matters.

fifteen

. . .

"I CAN SAFELY SAY I've never been as nerve-cited as I am right now." I press a hand to my stomach as Topher pulls the car to a stop.

"Nerve-cited?" He chuckles and angles in his seat to get a better look at me.

I may have had to dig at the back of my closet for the pink puffy jacket I'm currently sporting, along with a white beanie and matching scarf, but it still fits the same.

It's the woman inside who's different. "Nervous and excited."

"Ah, of course." He flicks a look to the back seat. "How you doing there, Fred, old boy?"

The rental company accidentally gave us a four-door car with a tiny back seat, into which Frederick is crammed along with several gift bags—presents for my family. His knees nearly reach his chest and he's hunched over like Quasimodo.

When we asked the rental company for our original reservation, they apologized profusely. After all, it's New Year's Eve and a lot of people travel this time of year, so their stock is low. We could have thrown Topher's name and title around, but we take advantage of the anonymity whenever possible.

Over the last week, there have been plenty of photo ops. We've been trending on social media, but there are only a handful of haters. Most of the people out there are actually cheering for "Christophen"—the couple name they've given us—to succeed. I know the news scrutiny we face won't always be this positive, but I'm certainly not going to complain when it is.

"Simply splendid, mate," Frederick says. "And no, I don't at all feel like I'm going to vomit with the way you drive."

"It's the Manhattan traffic, Freddy." I turn and give him a friendly squeeze on the kneecap. "You'll get used to it."

He mumbles something under his breath and Topher and I laugh.

Then I remember where we are and my breath catches once more.

"It's going to be all right, love." Topher takes my hand and brushes a kiss there. "Whatever happens, I'm right beside you."

"Together."

"Exactly."

I nod, inhaling courage from him. It's only been a week since we declared our love for the world to see, but our relationship has already grown by leaps and bounds. It just goes to show that some people need four years to know they've found the One.

For us, it only took four weeks. (Fine, probably less.)

And though the last week has been full of relaxing— first with Topher's family (before they flew back to Kentonia to host their New Year's celebration) then my friends (including Evie and Connor, who returned a few nights ago from their Jamaican honeymoon)—it's also flown by.

Still, it's given me plenty of downtime to contemplate what's about to happen … ever since I read the text from my sister.

The one offering me forgiveness, saying she's been praying for me to come home since the moment I left.

I tell you, she's better than all of us.

I can't wait to get my arms around her. Mom, though … I won't be surprised if we show up to a horde of photographers or at the very least a camera set up to record my homecoming. Especially since I'm bringing royalty with me.

We climb from the car and the icy New York wind slices through me as I hold onto the vehicle to avoid slipping on the frozen sidewalk. Topher rounds the car and takes my hand, and Frederick walks silently behind as we make our way to the door of the historic townhome in front of us.

My fingers itch to take a photo of the house, because it —and this moment—represents so much. Good memories and bad, this is the home I've been running from. The stairs are dusted with snow, a little mud mixed with the white to create sludge. But only just a tad. It creates a striking contrast next to the elegant brown sandstone, manicured greenery, and classic windows with gorgeous framing.

Without hesitation, I pull my phone from my purse and snap away. Topher stands back, understanding my need. He's been so patient with me, so encouraging. He's the reason I signed up for a photography course to begin in a few weeks.

The reason I finally made my social media feed public.

He makes me brave.

Brave enough to face whatever is waiting for me on the other side of that tall door.

Stuffing away my phone, I rub my hands together again, walk up the stairs, and knock. Topher joins me just before the door swings open.

And there she is—my beautiful little sis.

"Hi, Sam."

Her lips quiver. "You're really here."

"I'm sorry it took me so long."

She shakes her head. "I'm just glad you finally made it." Then she's tugging me inside and into an enthusiastic hug as if nothing bad ever happened between us, and I aim in that moment to become more like her.

It takes me a minute to notice that we're both crying, and I pull away to peek behind her. The brownstone's living room is decorated to the nines as always—a full Christmas tree resplendent in its trimmings, garland lining the staircase railing, designer stockings hung on the mantel.

But wait. There are not just two.

There are three. No, wait. Four.

Did they hang stockings for Topher and me?

And that's when I see her—Mom. She's standing in the corner of the room, simply staring at me as I take it all in. Her hair is a bit thinner and she's got little wrinkle lines around her eyes and mouth that weren't there before. She's not in her finery like I expected, especially given she's meeting a prince. There are no diamonds or pearls or silk hosiery or coiffed hair. She's wearing dress slacks and a simple long-sleeved blouse—still elegant, but less formal.

And she's got her hand pressed to her mouth, tears leaking from her eyes, which are glued to me.

I take another breath and step around Samantha. "Hi, M-mom. I'm home."

With those words, my mother loses it. We're talking a heaving bosom, loud sobs, the works.

I glance around, squinting. Where are the cameras?

As if sensing my thoughts, Samantha leans in, whispers. "It's just us. Mom's changed. After you left … she never forgave herself, you know."

No, I didn't know. Because I ran. I hid.

But now? I'm running toward my family, not away.

I open my arms and my mom rushes forward. "Lauren." She buries her face in my hair, inhales. "Oh, baby. I'm sorry."

"Me too, Mom. Me too."

This is honestly more than I ever hoped for. And I'm not so disillusioned to believe there won't be some deep and gut-wrenching conversations to come. But as I look up over Mom's shoulder, I catch a glimpse of Topher. He's watching me, his eyes dancing.

And when he mouths, "I love you," I smile, nod. Mouth back, "Me too."

Then he turns to give Samantha a hug, and I pull away from Mom. "You know what sounds good?"

She takes a strand of my hair and plays with it, pressing it back behind my ear. This is the mom I used to know. Maybe she's finally back, to stay. "Hot chocolate? With extra whipped cream?"

"How did you know?" I shoot her a silly smile.

"Because, daughter of mine, some things never change."

That's true. Some things never do. And others? They change with the passing of the wind. Like Topher said, we don't know what the future holds. But if we keep holding hands with those we love no matter what, this life will be a good one.

And while these days might feel like the best of my life, I know there are more still to come.

Giddy up—because here we go.

epilogue

. . .

Shelby

I **LOVE** three things in this world more than life itself:

1. My friends and family (counted as one because my friends feel like family)

2. Musicals (especially those produced in the 1960s—think *The Music Man* and *My Fair Lady*)

And 3. My best friend, Eric Moody

The first two are no surprise to anyone who knows me.

The third is a secret I'll carry to my grave.

I am usually able to keep my love for Eric under lock and key. A simple fisting of my hands or finding a distracting task or thinking about all the reasons it would be impossible for us to be together—those things help most of the time.

But other times, it's much harder.

Like right now, on New Year's Eve, as I watch him play charades with my family. He looks so silly—one arm stretched high overhead scratching his head, the other tickling his belly as he ape-walks in front of everyone—but his confidence is magnetic.

And that's not just because I wish I could claim the same for myself.

But there's something so wonderful about a man who doesn't take himself too seriously.

He's also entirely too handsome for his own good, with a lean figure that's not devoid of muscle, brown hair that's adorably mussed, and blue eyes that have been sparkling with mischief since we met at the age of nine. That was just after my mom was diagnosed and Eric had been shipped to yet another foster family.

Ever since then, he's become a part of mine. We've adopted him as one of our own. He's at every family function, and sometimes I wonder if my family prefers his company to my own.

Not that I blame them. He's pretty great.

Guesses fly from every direction—my dad joins in, as do my stepmom, two of my brothers, and four of my nieces and nephews.

"The Grinch!" My oldest nephew, Dylan, shouts his guess at the top of his lungs.

My sister, Deb, covers his mouth with her hand and laughs. "Not so loud, crazy kid."

Not so loud? Who is she kidding? This is the loudest family in the history of families, and that's not just because there are six of us kids.

All of them married with kids—except me.

Eric walks to Dylan and starts pretending to pick and eat bugs off of him. Why has no one got the right answer yet? "Monkey," I say. I'm on the other team, and

I'm not supposed to be guessing, but I can't help myself.

No one seems to hear me—not surprising, since I'm the quiet one of the group.

No one except Eric, that is.

He stops what he's doing, looks at me, and grins, then lifts his hands overhead like he's just scored a touchdown. "We win!"

"What? How? What was the answer?" Calls of confusion go up.

He points at me before sashaying to the whiteboard and adding the winning tally to his team's side. "Shelby guessed monkey."

"Aunt Shelby!" My ten-year-old niece Delilah throws her hands on her hips like the little sassy pants she is. "You weren't even on their team!"

"Sorry," I squeak. Taking a throw pillow off the couch, I bury my face in it while the room explodes into friendly arguments over technicalities and who really won.

Finally, someone says it's almost time for the midnight countdown and I hear lots of rustling, feel the release of couch springs as people stand and shuffle off. When I peek up, I find myself alone with Eric, who's leaning against the fireplace mantel, all cool and casual, just grinning at me. "Didn't like being the center of attention there, huh?"

"Do I ever?"

And like it's nothing (because it's not, to him), he joins me on the couch, tossing an arm around my shoulder and squeezing. "No, but thanks for speaking up and putting me out of my misery. If they didn't guess it soon, I was going to have to somehow mime the flinging of poop—and no one wants to see that."

I swat at his chest and toss back my head in laughter. "Eric, gross."

This is us, fully comfortable with each other, able to talk about anything.

Anything, that is, except the expectations that practically everyone in our lives has for us. My friends think they're coy with their insinuations and teasing. I've heard the guys rib Eric too. Heard him assure them we're just friends.

And we are. That's all we ever can be.

It doesn't matter that I'm dying a little inside right now as the scent of his warm orange-vanilla cologne wafts over me and the tips of his fingers play with the ends of my hair. He doesn't mean anything by it.

But it means everything to me.

Even though it shouldn't. It can't.

Before I can dig my fingernails into my palms as a reminder, my family waltzes back in holding sparkling cider (for the kids and my two pregnant sisters-in-law) and champagne (for the rest of us) in clear plastic cups. My stepmom, Frannie, stoops and presses one into my hand, then gives Eric one too.

Someone turns on the television, where there's a replay of the ball dropping in New York. I smile at the memory of the text I received a few hours ago from Lauren, who's there with her family. They had a wonderful day together and she sent me an adorable shot of her and Topher beside her family's tree, kissing at midnight.

And as the countdown starts and my rowdy, lovable family shouts along—"Twenty-nine, twenty-eight"—I feel Eric's eyes on me.

Turning my body toward him, I make a face. "What?"

"Nothing." He's unusually quiet.

I nudge him with my shoulder. "Thinking about work?" We have to return on Monday. He's a teacher like me, and the two-week break has been nice.

"Nineteen, eighteen!"

He shakes his head as his eyes roam my face. Something unfamiliar wends through me. Sometimes I catch him watching me, but never this intently.

I swipe at my cheek. "Do I have leftover pizza on my face or something?"

"I would have told you *that*."

"I know." I squint. "You okay?"

"Just thinking."

"Ten, nine, eight!"

He lifts his glass, then presses the lip of it against the lip of mine. "To the year ahead."

This is our tradition. Year after year.

I smile, battling the thought that I can't take another three hundred and sixty-five days of being his best friend—and only his best friend. But we can never be anything more, because … well, *reasons*, all right?

So I suppose I'll take what I can get, even if denying my feelings gets harder with every passing year.

"Three, two!"

"And everything it might bring," I whisper, concluding our private toast.

The room explodes into cheers and shouts of "Happy New Year!" Around us, I'm sure all the couples are kissing. They always do.

If I had my heart's deepest desire, someday Eric and I would join them.

But that's never going to happen. I won't let it.

I won't sacrifice Eric's dream for my own.

So instead of leaning forward and kissing him like I really want to do, I merely maintain eye contact with my best friend, slip on a fake smile, and sip my drink.

Because this is as good as it's going to get.

Gah! It was so fun revisiting some of my favorite fictional people. I hope you've enjoyed reading the stories of this group of friends as much as I love writing them. I'm so excited to give Eric and Shelby their own happy ending in *Belonging With Her Best Friend*.

If you enjoyed Topher and Lauren's story, would you consider leaving a review?

Also, if you'd like to join my newsletter for updates on my other books, book recommendations, deals, give-aways, and more, sign up at www.KristinCanary.com/subscribe.

sneak peek

Belonging With Her Best Friend

I can think of a thousand things I would rather endure than the moment I'm living in right now.

Sky diving (that seems obvious). Going on *The Amazing Race* (how stressful does that show look?). Getting thrown up on by all thirty of my kindergarten students—at once.

Telling my best friend, Eric Moody, that I love him.

Okay, maybe not that. Definitely not that.

But standing here backstage—my arm around the lovable yet slightly snot-nosed Rosa Johnson—while director-slash-theater-teacher Sonia Riverdale stares at me, her jaw dropped, is nearly as terrifying.

"Why, Shelby Phillips." The fifty-something with bleached blonde hair throws a well-manicured hand on a voluptuous hip. "You've been holding out on us."

I swallow, my gaze darting this way and that. We're now amassing a small crowd—mostly made of tiny people, sure, but still. They don't need to know that their stage manager can sing. It's irrelevant to them. And oh so embarrassing for me.

"Um." I cough. The overhead lights glare down on me, like a spotlight I don't want. Despite the air conditioning inside the K-8 school, my armpits begin to itch. "I don't know what you mean."

Little Rosa tugs on the bottom of my tank top. During the school year, I wouldn't dress so casually at work, but it's the summertime, and all forty or so people who are currently in the building are here working on Redmont Ridge's summer musical theater show, *Cinderella.*

Ignoring the weight of all the eyes on me, I squat to the six-year-old's level and squeeze her arm. "Yes, sweetie?"

"Thanks for singing with me." The smile she flashes holds no trace of the tremble from minutes ago, when I came upon her as she paced back and forth backstage, crying. "I think I know the right notes now."

A moment of peace wends through me. I suppose it was worth any embarrassment to help such sweetness shine. "Of course. Happy to help."

"You didn't just help." Sonia studies me as I stand again. "You inspired! You have a lovely voice. Why have I been relegating you to props and backstage management all these years when you've got those pipes on you?"

"That's where I like to be." And this is why I only ever sing in the closet, where I'm surrounded by jackets and sweaters to muffle the sound. Well, that and the shower. But that's not so weird. Everyone sings in the shower, right?

The point is, I do not perform in front of others—not since that memorable audition when I was twelve. But today, I broke my rule.

At least it was for an adorable reason.

Speaking of that reason, Rosa skips across the mostly empty stage to join a few friends who are occupying the auditorium's folding theater seats. Thankfully, the crowd has started to disperse, apparently bored by now. The ten or so adults who are either cast members or volunteer helpers are nowhere to be seen, while the kids —kindergartners all the way up to middle schoolers— continue taking advantage of our fifteen-minute rehearsal break. They practice dance steps, drink from colorful water bottles, play tag.

They're not affected in the least bit by what just happened. *Their* hearts probably aren't still sprinting at an unstoppable speed.

They aren't afraid to face the director.

But then there's me.

Sonia takes one more step in my direction, tapping her chin. "Don't think you're getting out of a lead role in next summer's show."

"Oh. Um." Is that all I know how to say? How about *"No way in the world will I ever get up on stage and sing again, thank you very much"*?

Unfortunately, I don't say things like that. Not out loud, anyway. Maybe I can simply fail to sign up to help with the show next year. I mean, sure, I've helped every one of the four summers since I've been a teacher here at the same San Diego school I attended myself. But I could take a—

Nope. Sigh. I know myself. I just can't do it. First of all, the summer arts program is always desperate for volunteers. Second, I love a good musical the way my housemate and friend Lauren loves 'N Sync. (Note: That's a lot. Like, she'd donate a kidney to Justin Timberlake if he asked for one.)

But perform? Sweat's breaking out on my forehead just at the thought of it.

Still, I have a whole year to practice saying no.

No. No. No. See? I can do it. I've got this.

Sonia gives me a nod—like it's a done deal—and walks away. So maybe I don't got this. My chest collapses as I inhale giant gobs of air.

Then someone slips an arm around my shoulders and said air is tinged with orange-vanilla cologne.

And once again, all is right with my world.

"Everything okay?" a low voice whispers in my ear.

I glance up at Eric, who is sporting his worn blue Padres hat backward. "Fine. Why?"

"No reason." He tugs the ends of my short blonde hair. "You just looked like a fish."

"A fish?"

Eric makes a face at me—bulging eyes, mouth in a round O. Then he sticks a hooked finger in the side of his mouth and tugs sideways.

Giggling, I shove him away. "That's so flattering. Thanks."

His blue eyes spark with mischief as he laughs and pokes me in the side.

I look around. "Where were you, anyway?"

"Painting sets just outside, of course. That's the job I was voluntold to do, remember?" He waggles his eyebrows at me.

My cheeks heat a bit. Yes, I may have begged him to help out this summer—and that would make me completely pathetic, except he's a middle school history teacher here as of last year, so it was totally legitimate for him to help out the arts program.

And spending time helping with a children's musical every day is exactly what every twenty-six-year-old man wants to do with his summer vacation, I'm sure. Ha. But Eric's a good guy.

The best guy.

Ugh. There I go again. I seriously *have* to find a way to get over him, or I'll be miserable for the rest of my life. And it's not as simple as writing him out of my life altogether. We've been best friends for seventeen years. My family is his family. My friends are his friends. And my life would be far *more* miserable without him in it.

"Yoohoo, Earth to Shelbs."

"Hmm?" Oh shoot, he's looking at me expectantly. I must have missed something. "How are the sets coming?"

"Fairly splendid, if I do say so myself."

"So modest." Though I'm honestly not surprised since Eric worked construction for seven years while putting himself through college. He's been teaching for a year.

"I only speak the truth." He bends his hand toward his chest, huffs on his fingernails, and scrubs them across his chest—which is currently covered in a tight blue paint-splattered T-shirt that's doing him all sorts of favors. His naturally athletic frame is exactly what I find attractive in a man. That, along with his brown hair that always has that adorably sexy "I just rolled out of bed" look, pretty much means he's the most handsome man I know. And his fun and sweet personality only makes him more good-looking.

But our years together have put me squarely in the friend zone—and even if Eric *did* want more, there are reasons we could never be. And while the thought of never being more than his best friend crushes my soul, all I need to truly be happy is for *him* to truly be happy.

And I know that, with me, he never really could be.

So I tolerate the zings of pleasure every time he touches me. The twisting of my heart whenever his smile is directed my way. The way warmth spills through my whole being when he sees me—really sees me—even when no one else does.

Like now. He's looking at me, a bit more seriously, head cocked to one side. "All right, what happened? Did Sonia say something rude? Because I will—" He makes a fist, hits it against the palm of his other hand, nods. "Well, not really, because I'm a gentleman and she's a woman. But I will have some seriously cutting words for her if she was mean to you."

"Stop." I tug his hands down, gripping them between my own. "I'm fine."

"Of course you are. You're the fabulous Shelby Phillips. The pied piper of small children. Men and women alike are putty in your hands!" His hands burst from my grip in a sweeping gesture. "Behold!" His voice raises and shouts as if thousands are listening to him.

Like always, he's got me grinning like a fool even as I'm rolling my eyes. "I've got to get back to work. And so do you. Those sets won't paint themselves." I start toward the props table, where I left my clipboard when I saw Rosa crying earlier. We pass a few kids leaning against a wall who are playing something on their tablets. They ignore us.

"Aw, come on, Shelbs." Eric keeps pace with me, pinching my elbow like a charmingly annoying dog nipping at my heels. "You know I hate painting with a passion. Give me a hammer and nails—good. A saw and sander. Even better. But the paint! Oh, the paint!"

"You're so dramatic. *You* should be the one Sonia's trying to get to perform."

"Wait, what?" He tugs on my arm, stopping me in my tracks and whirling me to face him. "That's what she wanted?"

"Yep." I wrinkle my nose. "Well, sort of." Snatching up the clipboard, I take a peek at my watch. Two more minutes till Sonia—who can be a fine arts drill sergeant when she wants to be—calls us to the stage again. Then I turn back to Eric, who is standing there with arms crossed over his chest, clearly still waiting for an answer. "She heard me singing, okay? I was helping Rosa with one of the songs."

A funny look comes across Eric's face. His jaw flexes a bit, his eyes widen ever so slightly, and he swallows. "You … sang? Like, in public?"

"Please don't make a big deal about this."

"But it is a big deal, right? You never sing. Ever. Like, every time your family does karaoke, and I beg you to duet with me, you wave your hand and tell me to sing my heart out. Which, of course, I do."

"You do." And it's always a sight to see him up there with my gaggle of nieces and nephews, wailing in the most awful falsetto along with Journey's "Don't Stop Believin'," jamming out like he has no qualms about failing in front of a crowd.

He and I couldn't be more opposite in that way, but it's one of the things I love about him. He just doesn't care what other people think—and I don't mean in an inconsiderate way. More in a "life's too short" way. And I get it. As a former foster kid who first lost his adoptive parents in a tragedy and then was carted from home to home after that, he's lived a lot of life. Much of it not good.

My life hasn't been a picnic either, but I don't have nearly the same seize-the-day courage that Eric does.

"I even use my adorable puppy dog eyes to try to get you to agree, but no dice." Eric leans in close, lowering his voice. "Now I know your secret."

I suppress a shiver. Because if he ever *did* know my real secret … "And what's that?"

"You leave me no choice but to persuade one of your million nieces or nephews to help me convince you to sing at the next karaoke party. Children are your weakness. I don't know why I didn't think of it before."

"Won't work." I'm saying the words, but without

much conviction, because let's be honest—I'd be hard-pressed to say no to a kid. Especially one I'm related to.

Eric rubs his hands together, glee written all over his face. "Challenge accepted."

"You'd better n—"

At that moment, Sonia claps and we all scurry back to the auditorium, snagging seats so she can discuss what else we need to accomplish today. It's a lot, but with only a month left until the show opens (we've been at this about two weeks so far), there's still a fair amount to do.

When she calls the ensemble onto the stage, I decide to stay in my seat for a different view than I normally have on the sidelines. Sonia sometimes likes for me to watch from the audience and give her notes afterward, and it's not a problem because my assistant stage manager can handle things alone backstage for a bit.

Eric stays beside me too, his upper arm pressing against mine as we watch the cast practice one of the opening numbers they learned earlier this week. It's not terrible, but we've got a long way to go. I make some mental notes to help some of the younger ones cement the steps in their minds a bit better.

The scene shifts and now the prince is onstage talking with his parents. Sonia purposefully gave the roles with the most lines to adults, so hilariously, the prince is being played by a new teacher, Rob Stevens, while the king and queen are two seventh-graders half his size. I tap my foot along with the next song, lost in the story in the same way I've always been since my mom introduced me to movie musicals at the tender age of six—three years before she was diagnosed with a rare genetic disease that took her life two years later.

Of course, I grew up seeing her perform in live shows. She was dazzling, commanding the stage with her presence and her beautiful voice. I so wanted to be like that, but the one time I got brave enough to try …

I can feel Eric's eyes on me and turn. "What?" I whisper.

The corner of his lip turns upward. "It's just fun watching you." He says it in the same teasing way he always does whenever we watch *The Music Man* or *The Sound of Music* or any number of classic musical movies and I'm inevitably enraptured. "You're adorable."

Adorable. Just what every woman wants to be called by the man she's crazy about.

I tuck a piece of hair behind my ear and shrug. "I just love it."

He squeezes my knee twice before letting go. "I know."

I ignore the tremor pressing up my spine thanks to his lingering touch. We both turn our attention back to the stage, where the teacher playing Cinderella is doing her scene with the Fairy Godmother—nine-year-old Betsy McGrath. I had Betsy in my class as a kindergartner my first year teaching and she's just as boisterous and animated as I remember.

And that's why I really shouldn't be surprised when she accidentally flings her wand across the stage. But I gasp when it tumbles and twirls right into the eye of Cinderella—Janice Lovegood. Poor Janice staggers backward, clutching her eye … and promptly falls off the stage into the orchestra pit below.

Eric jumps up from his spot beside me and races toward the stage while I just sit there, gripping the armrests, my heart screeching to a halt. Kids are screaming and rushing toward the edge of the pit to look over, while Sonia raises her hands and claps again in an attempt to commandeer their attention.

My gaze finally lands on Betsy, whose wide eyes are filling with tears. Oh no. I stand and hurry to the side ramp, taking it up to the stage and pulling her into my arms, shushing her and telling her it'll be okay.

"Sonia, you'd better call for an ambulance." Eric's voice drifts upward from the pit. "I think Janice might have broken her leg. We shouldn't move her."

Sonia whips out a phone. "Did she hit her head?"

"Thankfully, no. Doesn't seem like it."

"Hang on, Janice," Sonia calls, then pivots to hurry backstage. Probably so she can hear. The entire auditorium has broken out into pandemonium, and someone has to take charge.

I'm not normally that kind of person, but I wrangle six-year-olds for a living, so I can do it if need be.

Thankfully, I'm not the only adult here. There are a few parent and staff volunteers, plus Rob—aka The Prince—who jogs over to me. We've only spoken a handful of words to each other, but that doesn't matter now. He's also gone into teacher mode. "What's the plan? Should we have parents come early to pick everyone up?"

I bite my lip, considering. "Sonia might like to

resume practice after Janice is transported to the hospital. How about we take everyone out to the playground for a bit?"

He flashes me a thumbs-up. "Sounds good." Rob starts getting the few other adult volunteers' attention while I move to inform Sonia what's going on. She's still on the phone, however, so I take a moment to peek over the orchestra pit edge at Eric. He's sitting on the ground beside Janice, holding her hand and cracking jokes to get her to smile despite her obvious pain. He glances up at me, winks, then gives all his attention back to Janice.

I can't help the flutter in my chest.

"Shelby."

Pivoting, I find Sonia behind me, tapping her phone against her left palm. "Is the ambulance on the way?"

"Yes. I need to go meet them out front. And Janice's husband is going to meet *her* at the hospital." She stuffs her phone into the back pocket of her chinos and pinches the bridge of her nose. "I can only pray she doesn't sue the school."

Is that really what she's worried about? I place a hand on her upper arm. "I don't know Janice all that well, but she doesn't seem the type to sue. Everyone knows it was an accident." I take a beat before continuing. "Rob and I thought we'd take the kids to the playground, give the emergency crew room to work. Unless you want to just end practice?"

"I hate to lose a day of rehearsal, but I want to ride over with Janice. Leave no man—or woman, rather—behind, and all that."

"I completely understand. I'll have the children call

their parents to come to get them early, and I can stay with any kids whose parents we can't get ahold of."

"Perfect." Sonia tilts her head. "Walk with me, will you?"

"Just give me a minute." I jog back to Rob, let him know Sonia's decision, then tell him I'll be right back. After I rejoin Sonia, we start toward the side ramp and down into the auditorium, moving toward the back.

The director continues. "I'm no doctor, but I'm guessing this might put Janice out of commission for a while. She very likely won't be able to do the show."

"That's terrible. Hopefully it's not as bad as it seems. She makes such a good Cinderella." I push open the door from the auditorium into the theater building's foyer. The rays from the early July warmth—even in the summer, San Diego stays fairly temperate at only seventy-something degrees—travel through a bank of windows across from us as we amble through the empty space toward the doors that let out into the parking lot.

"She does. But do you know who *else* would make a good Cinderella?" The crash of the push bar echoes through the foyer as Sonia opens the door to the outside.

I purse my lips and step onto the walkway. A light salt-tinged breeze teases my hair, a reminder that we aren't that far from the ocean. "I'm not sure. The only other adults in the show are Juliet"—who is playing the Wicked Stepmother—"and ensemble members."

"The person I have in mind is not currently *in* the show." Sonia casts me a side glance.

In the distance, the whirr of an emergency vehicle grows louder.

"Oh!" I nod. "Samantha Quincy would be ..." Oh wait. The fifth-grade teacher can't do it, can she? "But she's on a long vacation and won't be back in town until right before school begins again."

"This person is quite available." Sonia smiles at me, eyebrows raised.

An ambulance speeds into our parking lot. Its siren punctuates my thoughts, giving me a sudden headache. Sonia can't be saying what I think she's saying. "You don't mean—"

"I do." She takes my hands in hers. "You would be the ideal Cinderella. You're petite, sweet as apple pie, blonde—and girl, can you sing! Plus I know you've already learned the music and the dance steps so far just by watching us."

"B-but seeing them and doing them are two different things. And I don't know all the lines." Not to mention the fact that I DON'T SING IN PUBLIC.

"So you'll learn them. You have a month."

"But—"

"Hold that thought."

A man and woman jump from the ambulance and Sonia waves them over. "This way." She leaves me standing there on the sidewalk, and I'm pretty sure an angler fish has nothing on my dropped-jaw expression.

I don't move—can't move—until the paramedics carry Janice out on a stretcher. Eric and Sonia come out behind them, and once they have Janice settled in the back, Eric shoots me a wave and jumps in with Janice. He'll be good medicine for her.

Sonia, whose purse is slung over her shoulder, faces

me again. "I've got to go, but think about what I've said, all right? I'll text you with Janice's condition once we know more and we can go from there. Good? Good." Without waiting for a reply, she waltzes toward her Red Mustang.

"No, Sonia," I whisper to her shadow. "Not good. Not good at all."

books by kristin canary

California Dreamin' Series

Enamoring Her Amnesic Ex (prequel)

Loving the Ladies' Man

Desiring His Dating Coach

Saving the Secret Prince

Belonging With Her Best Friend

Engaging the Office Enemy

Needing the Next-Door Neighbor

Hallmark Beach Series

Beachside Kisses With My Bodyguard

about the author

Kristin is a wife and boy mom who functions best on peach tea and cookie dough ice cream. A desert dweller, she always has her eye on the next trip to a beach somewhere—and if she can't travel there in person, then you'd better believe she's going to write about it. Kristin is never fully satisfied with a movie, TV show, or book without a hefty dose of romance in it, and she's grateful to be living a true-life love story with her own crazy little family. Connect with her at KristinCanary.com.

facebook.com/kristincanary

instagram.com/kristincanaryauthor